John Creasey · Master Storyteller

Born in Surrey, England in 1908 into a poor family in which there were nine children, John Creasey grew up to be a true master story teller and international sensation. His more than 600 crime, mystery and thriller titles have now sold 80 million copies in 25 languages. These include many popular series such as *Gideon of Scotland Yard, The Toff, Dr Palfrey* and *The Baron.*

Creasy wrote under many pseudonyms, explaining that booksellers had complained he totally dominated the 'C' section in stores. They included:

> *Gordon Ashe, M E Cooke, Norman Deane, Robert Caine Frazer, Patrick Gill, Michael Halliday, Charles Hogarth, Brian Hope, Colin Hughes, Kyle Hunt, Abel Mann, Peter Manton, J J Marric, Richard Martin, Rodney Mattheson, Anthony Morton* and *Jeremy York.*

Never one to sit still, Creasey had a strong social conscience, and stood for Parliament several times, along with founding the One Party Alliance which promoted the idea of government by a coalition of the best minds from across the political spectrum.

He also founded the British Crime Writers' Association, which to this day celebrates outstanding crime writing. The Mystery Writers of America bestowed upon him the Edgar Award for best novel and then in 1969 the ultimate Grand Master Award. John Creasey's stories are as compelling today as ever.

INPECTOR WEST SERIES

Murder:
One, Two, Three

John Creasey

HOUSE OF
STRATUS

This edition published in 2014 by House of Stratus, an imprint of Stratus Books Ltd., Lisandra House, Fore Street, Looe, Cornwall, PL13 1AD, U.K. www.houseofstratus.com

Typeset by House of Stratus.

A catalogue record for this book is available from the British Library and the Library of Congress.

ISBN 07551-3610-1
EAN 978-07551-3610-0

Chapter One

Michael and Daphne

"Oh, darling," Daphne Mallow said, "aren't you coming to bed?"

Michael, her husband, leaned back in his arm chair, a comfortable arm chair made on modern lines, upholstered with a vivid red tapestry, which showed up strikingly against the off-white carpet and the off-white walls. For a small house, this was as modern as one could be. It belonged, inside at least, to the top of some mighty building in New York, or Stockholm, anywhere except in the English countryside. But it had "something", and it was comfortable.

It was even paid for.

"Darling," Daphne insisted, "aren't you?"

Michael just grinned.

She shook her head, very slowly, with pretended exasperation. It wasn't all pretence, perhaps, but the reality of it didn't go very deep. She loved looking at him as he was now – completely relaxed, long legs stretched out, wiry hair untidy with that attractive wave, almost the first thing about him which she had noticed.

Sometimes she had a sneaking kind of guilty thought: he was *too* good looking.

Could any girl be blamed for falling for him? And could he be blamed, if—

He pursed his lips in the shape of a kiss, and his eyes still mocked hers. His were blue, hers grey. This was the way he would often make her get up, move to him, kiss him. But she couldn't be sure that was what he wanted.

It wasn't.

He moved his lips, very slowly, and formed the word "No" with great deliberation. "I am not coming to bed."

"Oh, you brute!"

"On the contrary, the brute in me is being subdued for the time being," declared Michael. "I'm going to read for a bit, but you get to bed, sweet. You look very tired. I'll make you a milk drink."

"I'm not a *bit* tired!"

"You look worn out," he teased. "Shadows beneath the eyes, haggard lines at the mouth, faint wrinkles at—"

"I haven't, really, have I?" asked Daphne, in a sudden flurry of alarm. "Wrinkles, I mean. I'd hate—oh, you devil!"

But she laughed.

He could fool her almost any time he liked. She took him as she took life: literally. It wasn't that she lacked a sense of humour, was just that she had a simple, direct approach to living, and did a great number of things without really thinking. Fooling him and being fooled made life good. It was, most of the time.

Now, for instance?

She felt happier tonight than she had for several days, and that was because Michael was happier; well, free from whatever had been on his mind. He had been moody and almost irritable, and for the better part of a week any hint of good humour had been forced. It wasn't, tonight.

She could only guess what the trouble had been.

Money, most likely; and when she thought that, she added fiercely to herself: "Of course it's money!" He gambled too freely, and spent too much money on trifling but expensive presents for her, and she knew that he was often in debt. He seldom told her so, and didn't show her his bank account; he just paid a regular amount into hers, and left the housekeeping entirely to her. Three times he'd had to ask her to do without any money for a week or two. She'd always managed; but it had made her realise how near the bone he was.

If not money, then – a girl?

She fought against believing that. She had never had any proof, never anything which really convinced her that he did more than flirt. The trouble was that he was away so often; she wished he had any job but that of a commercial traveller.

Representative!

She sometimes wondered whether he was out more often by night than he need be. She just wasn't sure. One part of her mind told her that she didn't want to find out, but much of the time she felt a nagging uncertainty, especially when he was away. When he was home, like this, leaning back in the chair which seemed to have been made for him, she had hardly any fears at all. He seemed so happy with her, and looked so good; "good", that was, in the sense of being wholesome and likeable. The way he smiled, the way he laughed, the complete relaxation of his long, lean, virile body as he sat there, accounted for part of this; but she had to admit one thing.

She was never really sure what he was thinking; never quite certain what was going on behind those blue eyes, even when he was smiling.

All she knew was that she loved him desperately; an odd thought, even of the possibility of losing him, could hurt.

"What time is it?" she asked suddenly.

"Turn your head and look, lazy."

"I want to look the way I am looking," Daphne said. "I like the view."

He seemed startled, and sat up; then jumped up and crossed swiftly to her. She hadn't time to get out of her chair, one as large and as vivid as his. She had dark hair, as straight as hair could be but for a good hairdresser, and the creamy complexion that had gone out of fashion in the early days of Queen Victoria. She was just a little plump, and beautifully formed; she would have been ideal for a chocolate box or the chorus of the *Folies Bergère*.

Suddenly, he was leaning over her, his hands were upon her, his lips were on hers. Without a word, without a thought, only with thudding heart and a strange, almost frightening breathlessness, they were together. His hands were so gentle, yet he drew her from the chair, together they went out of the room.

Wind, cutting through a tiny opening at the top of the bedroom window, made the door slam.

They hardly noticed it.

Half an hour later, he got up, slid into a dressing gown, grimaced at her, and went along to the kitchen. She lay in a glorious state of drowsiness, listening to the wind, knowing that the sea must be raging furiously, wondering idly what it was like at Tony's cottage.

She liked the cottage.

In a way, she preferred it to this little house, but wishing and dreaming didn't hurt.

She forgot Tony and the cottage.

She was still drowsing when Michael came in, with a whisky and soda for himself and the milk drink for her, steaming hot and bubbly and creamy on the top. He flung her a wrap, as she sat up, yawning. She would be asleep within five minutes, with or without the milk drink, but he liked to fuss her, and she enjoyed being fussed.

She was flushed; lovely.

"You won't be too late, darling, will you?"

"A lot of difference it will make to you, you'll sleep like a log," he said, wrinkling his nose at her. "What we want are twin beds, poppet."

"No! Never!"

He laughed.

She found herself laughing, too. She thought how good he looked, with the old silk dressing gown loosely round him, and his long legs poking out, the flesh firm, the skin tanned to a pale brown. There wasn't a thing about him that she would ever want altered. Eyes, nose, mouth, legs, arms, lean, strong body – even the back of his head!

It was when they were like this that he occasionally talked more freely; confided, if he had any worries; told her that he didn't really want to talk about troubles with her, because he didn't like worrying her. If he guessed how desperately she wanted to share everything – but it was no use, he was never persuaded that she did.

The first time he had ever talked like that was after he'd fallen down a few feet of cliff, several years ago. He had been terrified, and shown it while he had been hauled to safety; he had told her, later, how he always feared physical injury. Other things had shown her that he hadn't much physical courage, but – she wasn't thinking about that, then.

Would he start talking tonight?

She almost hoped not, because she was so tired. The warm, steamy fumes of the drink had crept into her, her body was beautifully relaxed, she was glowing, without being too warm. If he got in beside her, they'd soon be sticky hot; but if he started to talk she would have to sit up and make herself open her eyes wide.

He stood up and took the cup.

"Bless you," he said. "'Night, sweet. I won't be too late."

He blew her a kiss, and went out, putting the light out from the door switch. In the darkness, she lay with her eyes closed and the warmth stealing about her; she always felt like this after he'd brought her a drink. She could see him, as clearly as if her eyes were wide open and he was in a brightly lit room. With the touch of recklessness in his expression, true gaiety in his eyes, he had a quality that could make her heart leap and then thump wildly with excitement.

It didn't, now.

She'd wake up in the morning, and he'd be beside her; or else he would be standing by the side of the bed with the morning tea tray. When he was at home he didn't mind getting up first, didn't mind helping out in any way, and he was usually completely natural – except during those bad spells.

Thank goodness this one was over. They'd have a wonderful weekend.

She went to sleep.

She didn't know that it was a drugged sleep.

Michael Mallow looked through two newspapers, while sitting in the arm chair, smoked three cigarettes, and heard a clock strike eleven. He didn't glance up. His order book lay beside him, but he didn't open it. For ten minutes, he leaned back, smoking and staring at the tiny electric clock let in the wall above the fireplace.

There were small recesses in all the walls, with delicate wrought iron work in front of them, flowers growing from these. Everything was bright, fresh, clean. Red predominated; the bright red colour of blood.

He looked round, slowly.

Then he got up, and went along to the bedroom. He stared down at Daphne for several seconds, although he could only just make out the shape of her head and shoulders; the dim light came from the hall. The curtains were drawn, and he left them like that. He picked up his clothes, made sure that he had a collar and tie, and went out. He'd left studs and cuff links in his shirt.

He lit another cigarette, and began to dress. When he had finished, he went into the hall and took a raincoat off the small, box like hall wardrobe. Outside, the wind was smacking at the door, and rattling it, but he knew that little short of an explosion would wake Daphne.

He went out.

The wind leapt and blew wildly through his hair. He smoothed the wiry mass down, his palm brushing over the back of his head. He did that several times, but it made no difference; at last he gave it up. The wind was behind him as he walked towards the shed at the back, where he kept his car, and Daphne kept her bicycle. Being behind him, it got under that wiry hair, and seemed to lift it straight up from the crown of his head. It was coming straight off the sea, and although it called for more balancing than usual, he made good progress.

It was twenty five minutes to twelve when Michael Mallow settled in the saddle, and started off.

The cottage he was going to visit was only two miles away, and the road was level except just the last few hundred yards; there, it rose sharply. If she went by bike, Daphne always had to push it up that last stretch.

The road was just a pale ribbon beneath the stars. He didn't put on the lights, front or rear. No one else was likely to use this road tonight, because it fed only the cottage and a village which was eight miles away over the cliffs but only four miles away across country.

As he drew nearer the cottage, the road ran close to the cliffs. Now, the wind merged with the mighty roaring of the waves. It was as if a thousand lions, wakened out of wanted sleep to sudden wrath, were bellowing and roaring at the same time. The strange, thwacking sound of waves smacking against the rocks, the seething, roaring tumult, the long drawn out and menacing hiss with which waves drew back, as if to get ready for another assault, had a hypnotising effect. The front wheel of the bicycle wobbled off as if it was being drawn towards the edge of the cliff.

The big rock which made a dark shape against the stars and marked Demon's Cove, rose out of the darkness, and then fell away. Here, Mallow got off the bicycle. He was gasping for breath, but didn't stand about for long. The lights were on at the cottage, as if Tony Rawson, who owned the cottage, was waiting to welcome him. The wind, suddenly capricious, lifted his hair straight up from his crown again.

The seas roared.

The light beckoned.

Soon, he was near enough to the cottage to hear the faint sound of music.

Then, he saw a man, near by; a man in the shadows.

Suddenly, he felt fear.

Chapter Two

Frightened Michael

Daphne Mallow woke up.

It was the kind of waking to which she was used; there were faint noises which penetrated the blanket of sleep, and insisted on getting a hearing. She didn't open her eyes at first. Michael was probably getting up. He might be coming in with the tea, and that would be a pity; she would love another few minutes here.

Laziness!

She opened one eye.

Michael was in the room, and it was broad daylight. He was fully dressed, and bending over a case which stood open on a small table by the window. He was putting something in the case. He kept looking out of the window, jerking his head up every time. He didn't look round at her for a long time, and she was so startled that all she could do was stare.

He was packing a suitcase, something he never did unless he had warned her that he would be away for a day or two.

This was Saturday; he was never away on Saturday.

His movements were quick and hurried; he was always a careless packer, and she usually did the job for him. Why was he packing? Why did he keep looking out of the window, as if frightened of what he might see?

He turned, to take something out of an open drawer, and saw her.

Now, her eyes were wide open. She lay on her back, only her face visible above the sheet. He stopped moving, and his hand was actually hovering above the open drawer, not dipping in, not coming out. She had never seen him look like that before, and it sent fear cutting into her. All the glow of the bed and all the snugness was gone, taking away thought of a few more minutes of sensuous comfort.

She opened her mouth stiffly.

"Mi—Michael," she whispered.

"How long have you been awake?" he asked. His voice was also pitched very low. He withdrew his hand from the drawer, and turned to face her, but he didn't come forward. The expression was still new to her; and frightening. It was like looking at a stranger; and being looked at by one.

This wasn't her Michael.

He repeated harshly: "How long?"

"I've only just—just woken up." She started to hitch herself up. "Michael, what—?"

"Don't ask questions," he rapped. "Don't—" He broke off.

She was halfway up on her pillows, by then, and her arms and shoulders were bare. He didn't look anywhere but into her eyes. She could just see the reflection of her face and creamy shoulders in the dressing table mirror, but she didn't see them; only Michael.

He looked desperately ill.

"I'm sorry," he muttered. "Didn't want to wake you. Meant to leave a note. I—I've got to go north. Special job, outside my usual territory." The lie was so transparent that it was a wonder he thought it worth uttering. "Have to drive all day today, and tomorrow. Must be—be in Glasgow first thing on Monday morning."

She didn't answer.

He shouted: "What's the matter, you deaf?"

"Michael—*Mike!* What's happened?"

"I've told you what's happened," he said hoarsely and roughly. "I've been called to Scotland, special business. If I pull it off, I'll be—" He stopped.

"What's *happened?*" breathed Daphne. She pushed the bed clothes back with a sudden, almost angry movement, and sprang out of bed. Long, white legs were close together, her small white feet touched the pink carpet. The nightdress she wore was loose about the waist, the ends of the tie strings hung down. "Michael, tell me."

"Don't get up! Don't—"

She reached him, and gripped his hands.

"What's happened, what are you looking like that for?"

His hands were cold, and his body was quivering; she had never known him like it. She recognised the brutality of his fear. His eyes were red rimmed and bloodshot, as if he had been drinking; and she could smell whisky fumes on his breath. He didn't snatch his hands away, but let her hold him, and he tried to meet her gaze.

"Please tell me, Mike. Tell me what it is."

He gulped.

"No, I—I can't," he said. "It—it'll be all right." With sudden strength, he snatched his hands free. "No! And you needn't worry, you just—just tell everyone I've gone away on special business. Understand?"

"Michael, I want to know what's happened." But her voice was taut and scared.

She was wide awake, she felt calm, and was determined to make him talk. She clutched at his arms again, and caught one – and then he raised the other, gripped her shoulder, and roughly thrust her away. He had never raised a hand against her before, had never even looked as if he might.

She went staggering back against the bed, and collapsed on it.

She didn't speak, just watched him incredulously.

"Listen to me," Michael said harshly, "I'm going away on special business. I've got to go away. I'll be back. You needn't worry. Whatever happens, just say I was called away. That's all."

She didn't get up; and she began to shiver, then to plead.

"Mike, darling, I don't care what you've done. I don't care what it is. I want to help you. Please tell me what's happened, and I will. I'll find a way. Don't run away from me like this."

He was throwing things into the suitcase. Then he turned round abruptly, caught his hip against a corner of the case, and knocked it flying. Shirts, socks, handkerchiefs, a brush, all his shaving things – everything was strewn about the room. The case itself fell on one side, swayed to and fro, and then turned slowly and snugly the right way up, with one pair of blue socks in a corner.

"Oh, God," Michael cried. "Oh, God!"

He raised his hands to his face and his head was bowed. He stood like that, and when she reached him and put an arm about him, he didn't move.

This time, she just waited.

When he was no longer quivering, she bent down, and began to pack the case, without lifting it to the table. She kept looking up at him. When he took his hands away from his face, she saw a new pallor. She felt quite sure that he hadn't slept; if he had his eyes would not look so dreadful.

She got up, although she was so badly frightened.

"I—I can't tell you now," he said slowly and huskily. "I just can't, Daff. Wish I—wish I could. But I've got to go away for a few days. When it's all blown over—" He stopped.

"When *what's* blown over?"

He didn't answer, but there was a different expression in his eyes, as if for the first time, he saw a gleam of hope. His lips parted. His teeth showed, very white. He put his arms out, and gripped hers, near the shoulders. His fingers bit into the softness of her flesh.

"Daff, I'm in a jam. I'm counting on you. You'll do—you'll do anything to help me, won't you? You'll do anything, because—you do love me, don't you?"

"Of course I do."

"Say you—say you'll do anything."

"Of course I will!" she almost shouted at him, "but how can I if I don't know what it's about? What happened? Tell me. I don't care, I'll do everything to help you, but I must know what it's about. Don't you understand, I must *know.*"

He was really hurting her arms.

11

"Listen, Daff. I didn't come home last night. That's it and all about it. I didn't come home. I—I telephoned to say I'd be away for the weekend. Never mind why, say I—say I said it was unexpected business. And I didn't come home." He was gripping her so tightly that the pain almost made her cry out, but he didn't seem to realise it. "Will you say that, Daff, if—if anyone asks questions?"

"Who *will* ask questions? And what about? Mike, let—let me go. You're hurting."

He snatched his hands away.

She folded her arms across her breast, and her long, white fingers rubbed the places where he had hurt so much; but she wasn't thinking about that, then.

"I can't tell you," he said. "It—it's better that you don't know anything. If you don't know, you—never mind! You—you might not hear anything until Monday. I shouldn't think you would." Another fresh hope had sprung into his mind, and he snatched at it, brightening, gripping her arms again. "Daff, you go away! Go and spend the weekend with your mother, just say I've gone away on business."

She said very slowly and very clearly: "I must know what has happened, Michael."

He drew away from her.

There was silence between them for what seemed a very long time. Suddenly they were strangers; and it seemed to Daphne that Michael also realised it.

His mouth tightened and his voice grew hard.

"Go and spend the weekend with your mother. If you don't, you'll be letting me down. I'll get in touch with you when I can. Just say I came home for an hour yesterday afternoon, then went off, and rang you late last night and said I wouldn't be home for the weekend. Say you haven't seen me since. Understand?"

"But you may be seen driving away!"

"I won't be seen," he said roughly. She knew that he realised the folly of saying that, but sensed that nothing she could say would make him tell her what she so desperately wanted to know. "I'll get in touch with you, soon. I expect I'll want you to come and join me. We'll see. It might all blow over. If it does—"

"*What might blow over?*" she flung at him.

The stranger who was her husband spoke wearily: "Daff, go and make me a cup of tea, and cut me a bit of bread and butter. Or make some toast. I'm in a jam, a really bad one. I don't want you to know anything about it, yet. It may never be necessary for you to. I hope it won't be, but—but I'm relying on you. Just say I telephoned and couldn't get home. That's all."

She hesitated, and then drew on a dressing gown and went downstairs. She didn't look round. It was chilly, and she felt as if she was walking into a cold room. The wind was still blowing, she could see the shrubs in the garden, bent beneath its force; it was making windows rattle, too, and howling down the drawing room chimney.

It was silent in the small kitchen, which was spick and span, bright blue and cream, with much chromium and stainless steel. Daphne switched on the toaster, put on the kettle, and cut some bread. She felt numb. It was the uselessness of arguing which affected her, much more than the fact that she had never seen Michael anything like this since – since that fall over the cliff. He had been frightened then, and he was frightened now. If he had broken down, and told her what it was, it wouldn't have been so bad; and when he had buried his face in his hands she had thought that he would explain. Then he had stiffened, and become quite determined; and there was nothing she could do or say to make him change his mind.

She recognised the cause of it: the ugly fear.

He came down, ten minutes later; she had poached two eggs and had them ready. Mechanically, he said thanks; mechanically, he sat down and ate and drank. It was then seven o'clock. By ten past, he was ready to go. Then he took out his wallet, which was flat and nearly empty. He looked up at her, anguished.

"Have you—any money? Cash, I mean."

For a wild moment she thought that if she said no, he couldn't go. That passed, very quickly. She didn't speak, but went to the bedroom for her handbag; she had eleven pounds.

He took it.

The suitcase was on the floor in the tiny hall, and he took his coat from the wardrobe cupboard.

She caught her breath.

"Mike, can't you—?"

He started to pick up the case, then dropped it, and took her in his arms. The fierce passion of his kiss told her how desperate he felt; it was like a goodbye of absolute finality. She could feel the pounding of his heart and knew the passion that was in him.

He drew back, still holding her.

"Daff, trust me. Do what I ask. Don't say I've been home all night, don't tell anybody."

He snatched the case, turned, and hurried through the kitchen to the back door. It was bolted. She heard him draw the bolts back noisily. The door opened. He stepped into the wind, which made his raincoat billow out, and staggered for a moment. Then, without looking round, he went into the garage.

Only two houses were near this house and the garage, both hidden by trees. But Daphne found herself thinking of them. She heard the engine start up. Then the garage doors opened. She didn't go out again; something told her that it would be a mistake. Instead, she went into the drawing room, where the red chairs looked very bright in the morning sun, and the walls seemed almost harshly white.

She stood at the window as Michael drove off.

She was very, very frightened.

She did not go to her mother for the weekend, but stayed at home.

Nothing happened, and nothing was said to hint at the reason for Michael's terror.

Then, on the Monday, she could stand the strain no longer; so she went up to the cottage on the cliff to see Tony Reedon, a family friend whom she thought she could confide in, and who might even know something about the mystery.

The cottage doors were locked, and a newspaper was stuck in the letterbox. She looked through the downstairs window and saw nothing unusual, except that the rooms were more untidy than

Tony usually kept them. That was puzzling, but not – at that stage – even remotely frightening.

By then, the edge of her own fears had been dulled a little by time. They nagged more than hurt, and at moments she looked at a photograph of Michael and seemed to see him as the stranger who had glared across the room. Everything was touched with unreality. She lived in a kind of nightmare world, in which tomorrow would be normal and bring release from tension, but today was filled with dread.

When she came back from Tony's cottage, the white house seemed starkly bright against the pale green trees beyond. The grass wanted cutting. Weeds were beginning to cover some of the flower beds with a sheen of green. She saw all this without really noticing it; it hurt to come home and to think that Michael might – might not be coming back.

She opened the door, stepped inside, and kicked against two letters on the mat. One was addressed to Michael, one to her. She picked up Michael's, first, and held it tightly; leaned against the wall, and then opened it. It was from Mildmay's London Office; his firm's. She saw the pale blue letter heading, the blue typing, the spidery signature at the foot: *H. J. Netherby*. It was only a few lines, but it affected her as a knife, stabbing.

Dear Mr. Mallow,
Instead of visiting Basingstoke on Tuesday, which is on your itinerary for this week, will you be good enough to come to London and see me? I have urgent matters to discuss about the south and south west. I shall expect you at 11.30 a.m.
Yours very truly,
H. J. Netherby

That spidery signature held her gaze for a long time. Then she glanced up swiftly at the date; *Saturday's*. She had never believed the story about Scotland, but here was the final, damning proof.

The letter was cold; like Netherby. She had seen him only once, and didn't particularly want to meet him again. Michael disliked

15

him. He had the aloof efficiency of a machine, it would be impossible to appeal to his better nature, to try to fob him off with an excuse if Michael didn't go.

It was like the last straw.

She could imagine Netherby sitting in his small office, in front of the small desk, with one hand out of sight, and the other, in its skin tight glove, resting on the desk. Perhaps the reason for Netherby's coldness was the fact that he had been severely injured; she didn't know how, and didn't know whether his black, shiny gloves covered artificial hands, or stumps, or paralysed fingers. They didn't look like flesh and blood, and somehow Netherby himself didn't. She couldn't expect help or understanding from him.

The bitter irony was so hurtful.

She didn't think Michael had been summoned to the London office like this for months. It was only a small office, the manager and three or four girls, but—

Damn Netherby!

It wasn't so easy to forget him. It was the finality of the letter which affected her so; Michael was to be there on Tuesday. Tomorrow. She didn't know where he was, she couldn't be sure that she would ever see him again.

She picked up the other letter, and suddenly felt colder than she had all the morning. It was addressed in pencil. It wasn't recognisable as Michael's writing, but couldn't he have printed it? She wanted to tear it open and snatch the contents out, but at first she could only stare.

It was so thick; much more than just a letter.

At last, she ripped it open, and shook it to get the contents out. A small bundle of one pound notes, kept together by a rubber band, slid on to her hand. She looked at that stupidly, then shook the envelope, then squeezed it so that the open end gaped, and peered inside, hoping that she would find a note from Michael.

There was none; only the money.

She stood with them in her hand, staring out of the drawing room window, dry eyed, but for some reason feeling the sharp edge of pain more than she had since Saturday morning.

Had *Mike* sent this?

She was still holding them tightly when a big green car drew up outside the house, and two men, big men, got out. They walked together up the short drive; one she had seen before, although she didn't know him. He was big, ungainly, and rather like a bull terrier to look at. The other, brisk moving, alert and good looking, was the one to catch her eye; he was a stranger.

It was the man she had seen before who drew ahead and, she knew, rang the bell.

She was standing with the money in her hand when the other moved suddenly, and looked through the window. His gaze lit on the notes. She should have hidden them, she—

She turned round slowly, to get the money out of the man's sight. With no good reason except the compulsion of her fears, she wanted to hide it. She looked round, wildly, then hurried from the room, ran into the kitchen, and pushed the bundle into the larder, behind a stack of sugar.

The front door bell was ringing.

She made herself go steadily towards the door, opened it, and hoped that neither of these men knew how fast her heart was beating.

The handsome one was in front. He had a brisk, no nonsense air about him, but there was something friendly in his manner.

Yet he sent her fear screaming.

"Good morning, Mrs. Mallow," he said. "I'm sorry to worry you, but can you spare us a few minutes? This is Superintendent Wortleberry, of the Mid Sussex Constabulary, and I am Chief Inspector West of Scotland Yard."

Chapter Three

Chief Inspector West

Chief Inspector Roger West could disarm most people, whatever their mood or their malice. It was part of his philosophy that in ninety nine cases out of a hundred it was better to talk to a witness who felt at ease than to one who felt scared. There were times to use scare tactics, but they had to be judged to a nicety.

This certainly wasn't one.

He liked the look of the girl. She wasn't much more, although Wortleberry had told him she had been married four years. That sleek dark hair and that creamy complexion and those grey eyes – she might have walked straight off a woman's magazine cover. She was quite tall, five seven or eight, and looked extremely well in a linen suit, wine red in colour, with a lot of pleats in the skirt. Beneath the jacket a cotton blouse was white and starched, and she wore a skullcap of wine red feathers.

She said: "What—what is it about?"

The fear still screamed in her: that it was about her Michael, that he was dead, or that he'd been arrested for some crime. Terror, not presence of mind, stopped her from blurting out: "Is it Michael?" Then instinctively she realised that she must let this man do the talking; she mustn't say a word.

Every instinct she had was deployed, then, in defence of Michael.

"It's about a friend of yours," West said casually. "Mr. Anthony Reedon."

She moved her lips, to say "Oh", and felt very weak. Then she moved aside, to let them come in. They seemed very big; massive. About the cumbersome Wortleberry there was a faint smell of beer and tobacco smoke, and perhaps the farmyard.

West did not appear to be studying her closely, but there wasn't much he missed. The fear, first, which clouded her mind and made her clumsy – when, for instance, she seemed to take it for granted that they knew which room to go in, and blundered into Wortleberry as he hesitated by a door. Then she began to speak too quickly.

"Oh, I'm sorry, this is the room. I'm afraid I can't help you, I haven't seen Tony for a week or more. Honestly."

That "honestly", thought West, was a clear indication of her nervous frame of mind.

But there could be plenty of reasons for the woman's nerves.

They went into the red and cream room. It had a startlingly fresh look, made vivid because the sun shone into the top of the big window at one end. The room stretched right across the little house, with a French window opening on to the back garden, the big lawn, and the copse beyond, a long, wide window overlooking the front garden with its small lawns, roses, and beds of flowers. The plants were still small and green; one bed of stalky wallflowers waited to be cleared.

"Won't you—won't you sit down?"

"No, thanks," said West, "I've just driven from London, and don't mind standing for a bit. When did you see Mr. Reedon, do you say?"

She still spoke too quickly.

"About ten days ago. When was it? A week ago last Thursday! Michael, I mean my husband, was home that Thursday, we went up to Tony's for a drink, it was such a lovely evening. We walked. He ran us back. I'm sure it was Thursday, I was so pleased that Michael was home a day earlier than usual."

"Isn't he home every night?" asked West.

He sensed Wortleberry's disapproval at the question; for the local Superintendent had already told him that Michael Mallow was a commercial traveller, on the road four or five nights a week, and a bit of a gay spark; in fact, Wortleberry had told West a great deal.

Wortleberry's trouble was that he might be tempted to let this girl, and perhaps other witnesses, suspect how much he knew.

"Why, no, he's a travelling representative," Daphne Mallow said swiftly. "He's with Mildmay's, you know, stationery and office equipment." She paused for a split second, and West sensed a quickening tension, picked out the slight change in her tone. "He's gone up to Scotland on a special job, hasn't been home all the weekend. I don't know what the job is, but he seemed to think it would mean promotion."

"Hmm," thought West. "So he's gone away."

Wortleberry was a snuffler; it wasn't a pronounced snuffle, really a kind of heavy breathing or wakeful snoring. West didn't know him well enough to guess whether the series of peculiar sounds then indicated scepticism.

"What's the matter, why are you interested in Tony?" Daphne asked.

Her tone was back to normal again. It was impossible ever to be sure, West knew, but he thought that this new change meant that whatever was on her mind, it didn't concern Anthony Reedon.

"We can't find out where Mr. Reedon's been lately," West said.

"You can't *find*—" She broke off, and then said sharply: "What do you mean? Has he gone away?"

"We hoped you'd be able to give us some information," West added easily. "Do you know where he is?"

"Why, no." She was much more natural and not at all worried about this subject, just a comely, smart young woman. "As a matter of fact I cycled up there this morning, but couldn't get an answer."

"Do you often go there during the day?"

Daphne stared, and Roger West saw her cheeks flush suddenly; she was reading an innuendo which he'd put in deliberately. But her answer was calm enough, if a little stiff.

"On nice days I sometimes cycle up for coffee, or a cup of tea. Mr. Reedon is an old friend of ours."

"Did you know he was going away?"

"I'd no idea."

"Did your husband?"

"If he did, he didn't tell me," Daphne said firmly.

Wortleberry was making those heavy breathing noises, undoubtedly thinking that West had thrown away the advantage. The young woman was much more collected, West could imagine him thinking; so you could never tell with these Yard men, in spite of their reputations.

West gave his most warming smile. That made him an arrestingly handsome man, with his fair complexion, corn coloured hair which curled a little; it looked crisp but wasn't wiry, like Michael Mallow's.

"Does your husband tell you everything, Mrs. Mallow?" he asked.

She flashed: "Of course he does!"

Roger passed that over smoothly, as if it really didn't matter.

"About Mr. Reedon, do you know if he has any other close friends in Hoole, or near by?"

"Well, I suppose he hasn't," the woman said. She poked a strand of hair. "He has a lot of acquaintances, but I don't think you'd say that many of them are close friends."

"Relatives?"

"I don't think he has any—certainly no close ones."

"Do you know what he does for a living?"

"Well—yes." She hesitated. "He's a kind of journalist, what do they call them? Free lance, that's it. He writes for the newspapers sometimes, and magazines."

"Is that all?"

"I've never known him do anything else," Daphne said. "I think—it's no business of mine, but I think he was left some money a few years ago, and threw up his job."

"Do you know what the job was?"

"No. In—in some office, I think."

"Do you know who left him the money?"

Daphne hesitated, then said: "No."

Wortleberry was almost silent, the snuffling stilled. Many men were silenced when they first heard West questioning a witness. The odd thing was that he gained his effect without raising his voice, without phrasing questions in any particular way. It was a kind of decisiveness, almost as if he were saying, "Now we've got to get on with this, let's have the truth quickly, please," and allied to it was a kind of natural charm. Getting to know West, one realised that his greatest single asset was his ability to win the trust of the most unlikely people.

His manner relaxed.

"Thank you very much, Mrs. Mallow. If you should hear from him, I'll be grateful if you'll let the Superintendent know." He smiled at Wortleberry. "You'll leave Mrs. Mallow your card, won't you?"

"Eh? Oh, h'm, yes."

Wortleberry searched inside the pocket of his loose fitting blue serge suit. He took out a card and handed it over.

West opened a cigarette case, fumbled, and dropped a cigarette. He bent down for it, while Wortleberry was handing the woman his card.

As well as the cigarette, West picked up a screw of paper, which was in his pocket before he stood up.

"Thank you," Daphne said to Wortleberry, and added formally: "I'm sure he'll be back soon."

"*Are* you?" demanded West, and somehow made the question sound as if he believed that she was lying.

It puzzled but didn't worry her, and she answered with complete simplicity.

"Well, yes, why shouldn't he?"

"I hope you're right," West said, and let his doubts sink in. "Mrs. Mallow, have you any reason to think that Mr. Reedon has enemies? Anyone who wishes him ill?" He hardly paused. "Had he ever talked to you about being alarmed, frightened, worried?" There was the briefest of pauses then, just to let her digest those questions; and next: "Did he take any special precautions against theft, or burglary, or physical injury?"

She must have felt as if she were standing outside on a blustery day.

"Why, no. I don't—I don't understand you. Why should he?"

West didn't answer.

Wortleberry rumbled deep in his throat.

West saw the surprise, almost bewilderment, in the girl's eyes as he flung out suggestion after suggestion, hinting at all manner of troubles. It confused her, and he saw the way she tried to keep up with him, as he flashed from one innuendo to another. After he'd said "physical injury" he cut his words off and closed his mouth sharply, lips compressed, eyes almost fiercely aggressive.

And after a moment's pause, all her colour ebbed, fear put a feverish glitter in her eyes, and she ejaculated: "Oh, so!"

Wortleberry shuffled his feet, and raised his hands slightly, as if he thought this was the moment they had been waiting for; the moment to pounce.

West said very softly: *"When* did you last see Mr. Reedon?"

"I—I've told you! Last week, no, the week before, it was—"

"When?"

"I've told you!"

"Were you at the cottage on Friday night?"

"On Friday? No!" she cried.

"Sure?" He was aggressive now, and frightening.

"Of course I am."

"Was your husband?"

"He—he couldn't have been, he wasn't home, he had to go to Scotland."

"Then how do you account for the fact that the tracks of your bicycle were found near Mr. Reedon's cottage today—tracks which must have been made Friday night or early Saturday morning?"

The question was as bewildering as it was frightening. Daphne didn't answer, just stood in silence, knowing that these men now felt sure that she was lying.

Chapter Four

Facts About Hoole

Daphne stood absolutely still, her face colourless and her eyes still feverishly bright. She began to breathe heavily. Obviously she wanted to look away from West, but couldn't bring herself to do it. The tension in the long, bright room was brittle.

"Well, how do you explain those tracks?" West was still aggressive.

"I—I—I can't."

"Were you up at the cottage?"

"No!"

"Was your husband?"

"I tell you he wasn't home!" she cried. That was the one thing she had to make them believe. All the anxiety about Tony was unimportant compared with that.

Then something made her ask: "How—how do you know that my bicycle was—was there?"

"The tracks, as I told you," said West briefly. "They must have been made just after the rain on Friday—they're quite distinct. The ground was dry by Saturday midday, in the hot sun."

"Oh," Daphne said weakly. "Well—I—I don't know. Someone—someone must have borrowed the bike."

"Did you lend it to anyone?"

"No."

"Sure?"

"Yes."

"Then why do you think someone borrowed it?"

"How else could it have got up there?" she demanded.

There was a long, tense pause; and in it, Daphne kept telling herself that above all things she must not let them know that Michael had been home on Friday night.

What had happened at the cottage?

Had Michael been—?

Suddenly, West smiled.

"Thank you for being so patient, Mrs. Mallow," he said. "If you should hear from Mr. Reedon, you'll let the Superintendent know, won't you?"

He turned away, as if quite satisfied after all.

Wortleberry seemed first startled, then surprised, and finally disapproving. He reached the door seconds after West, and watched the girl closely. Then he shrugged his big, sloping shoulders, and went after West, who had the front door open. Both detectives stepped on to the porch. The sun struck warm, and made the roses vivid, turned the grass to brilliant green. Not far off, the garden of another house was a mass of flowers almost hurtfully colourful. The beech and birch trees in the grounds of both houses and in the plots of land which carried *Building Plots For Sale* notices were all saplings. A few silver birch looked as if one had only to lean against them to break them in two. The leaves were light and bright, not yet grown to full size.

West smiled back at Daphne Mallow.

"Thank you again. Goodbye."

He put on his hat and turned and strode towards the car, reaching it well ahead of Wortleberry, who lumbered after him. The local Superintendent probably weighed three stone more than West's fourteen, but his height and breadth disguised the fact that he was nearly fifty inches round the waist; huge and truly ungainly.

Suddenly, West turned and hurried back, as if on the spur of the moment. Wortleberry saw the new anxiety in Daphne Mallow's face.

West might be pretty good, after all—

"Oh, Mrs. Mallow." West was brisk. "I hope it won't inconvenience you, but we shall have to take your bicycle. A man will be here for it, soon. We won't keep it longer than we must."

"All—all right," she said.

"Will it inconvenience you?"

"No. I—I can manage."

"May I see it now?"

"Yes—yes, of course."

It was near the garage; and seemed quite normal. West seemed to think so, too. So did Wortleberry, who had joined them. Soon, West beckoned a policeman who was out of sight of the house, said "Thanks," to Mrs. Mallow, and gave the policeman instructions to guard the bicycle until someone came for it from Hoole. Then West went back to the car and took the wheel. Wortleberry squeezed in beside him. Daphne Mallow stood at the open door, watching; she was thirty or forty yards away, and it was impossible to judge her expression.

The policeman was going round to the back; and the bicycle.

The small white house, its slate roof etched sharply against the background of trees, was built in stern, almost harsh lines; it was as out of place here as Reedon's cottage would have been out of place in a modern city. Yet the attractive, graceful garden took away from the starkness; creeper was starting to grow up the walls, and already saved the small garage from being such a blot.

"Nice looking woman," West said solemnly.

"Hm? Oh, yes. Beauty. Why didn't you—ah?" Wortleberry broke off, almost confused.

He was a throw back, West judged, and one of the better throw backs. Undoubtedly he stood a little in awe of the Yard, would behave with the greatest circumspection, and do exactly what he was asked – but beg leave to differ whenever he felt it important. He would always hesitate to question West's methods, although he'd been about to.

West was negotiating the bumpy, gravel road. Unmade roads abounded on the outskirts of Hoole, and this one was worse than most, with some big holes still half filled with water, although it hadn't rained for three days.

"Why didn't I try harder to make her crack?" West suggested.

"Well, hm, yes. Eh?"

"I think she's worried," West mused. "The idea of Reedon being hurt shook her badly. But her defences were up pretty quickly. Didn't you see that? I'd like to know a bit more before we have another talk with her—if one becomes necessary. Did you notice that money?" he added casually.

"What money?"

"I think you were ringing the front door bell," West told him. "When we arrived, she had a bundle of green one pound notes in her hand and was standing as if she didn't know what to do with them." He slid his hand to his pocket and drew it out again. "Care to unscrew that?"

It was a piece of thickish, manila type paper. Wortleberry took it from the palm of West's hand, and unfolded it with great care. His movements were surprisingly quick and efficient, and his hands small and pale. He held the paper by the corners, as he would anything which might need to be tested for finger prints; and the way he did this told West that Wortleberry would be exhaustively thorough.

"Envelope," he announced. "Addressed to Mrs. Mallow. Postmark London E.C. 3. Block lettering, lead pencil." He added almost to himself: "Shiny surface, good quality manila envelope. Mildmay manufacture?"

"I believe they specialise in that kind of envelope," West said, "but it's interesting, anyway. Just about the right size for a bundle of notes. It was in her hand when we drew up, she screwed it up and dropped it as she hurried out of the room. And the money was in her hand." He didn't draw any conclusions. "What did you think of her?"

"It's early to say. Eh?"

Yes, Wortleberry would be ultra cautious, too. He might become exasperating, but thoroughness was one of the major police virtues. And his men were good; like the chap, just a uniformed man, who had recognised the cycle tyre tracks as being similar to those made by Mrs. Mallow's bicycle.

"Going to see the body next?" he asked. He was leaning over to the back of the car, and fiddling; his huge chest pressed against West's shoulder. A moment later, he turned round and settled into his seat; he was then holding a newspaper and, with great care, he wrapped the crumpled envelope up in it. "Or the cottage? If you'd rather see the cottage, we ought to phone the office about Mallow being gone."

"We'll phone," West said. "I take it you know his car number."

"The local chap will," said Wortleberry.

There was a telephone kiosk not far along the road. Wortleberry squeezed in, and put through a call to his office. A general call was to go out for Mallow's car, a Vauxhall; and Mildmay's London office was to be telephoned, to check whether Mallow had been sent to Scotland.

"Ask the Yard to do that," ordered Wortleberry. "Just ask if they can contact him, don't raise any scare."

He nodded, a moment later; then rang off. He didn't speak until they were back in the car. Then: "Wonder why she did go to Reedon's cottage today."

"Aren't they genuine family friends?"

"Oh, yes, and she does go up there sometimes on her own. Nothing in it, though. Rumour'd get around if there were." Wortleberry was oracular. "Was she worried because she hasn't heard from Reedon, I wonder?"

"I didn't get the impression that she was worried about Reedon until the last moment, when she realised that he might have been hurt," West said. "Let's go to the cottage first, by the time we get back they ought to have finished the autopsy."

"Right ho," said Wortleberry. "Turn first right, then left, then second right. Only country lanes, you know, not made up. The cliff road's all right, though, when you get to it." The car was bumping over the uneven gravel surface and splashed through a pot hole. "They reckon it would put half a crown on the rates to make these roads up. Aren't enough people living out here yet to make road charges fair or worth while, either, so we'll have 'em like this for a few years longer. Nice view over Hoole, though, when we're up on the cliff."

"I don't know the town," Roger West said. "It looks pleasant, at first sight."

Wortleberry said smugly: "It's the nicest little sea coast town in the South of England. That's Hoole. Lived here all my life, and nothing's ever going to take me away." He fell silent and then asked, almost guiltily: "But talking of Reedon, he doesn't seem to have friends or relatives, does he? Mrs. Mallow said the same as I told you—lonely type of chap. Who'd want to kill him?"

"We'd better make sure it is his body," West said. "Second right you said, didn't you?"

"Yes, by that old stile."

The road climbed steeply for a few hundred yards, and ran through wooded land, where a soft mist of bluebells still lingered, although it was fading, most petals gone, the spiky green leaves flattening out. Birds flitted, or dived swiftly. Nothing else stirred. The wind had dropped, the sun was high, and it was hot inside the car. They turned off this road on to a narrow but tarred one, which had recently been surfaced with pale coloured washed gravel. The tyres crunched when West went close to the verge, where the gravel lay thick and loose. Grassland was on either side, now, but they could see the sea on the left and, in the distance, a sweeping bay with cliffs on the far side from here. A single yacht, its white sail looking startlingly white, rode the calm blue sea.

"Pull in at the top, and stop a minute," Wortleberry said.

West did so. There was plenty of room, and he went on to the short grass between the road and a tall rock, which looked dark and ominous in spite of the sun.

"That's Demon's Rock, guarding Demon's Cove," Wortleberry announced. "Wicked in rough weather, that cove. Let's get out a minute, I'll show you the lie of the land."

They got out. The breeze off the sea brushed their faces, the air smelt clear and fresh and strong; unfamiliar to a man from the petrol laden air of London.

They looked back the way they had come.

The town of Hoole, which had a population of nine thousand four hundred during the winter, and twenty nine thousand odd during the summer, lay in a valley between the hills which, in this part of Sussex, ran right down to the sea. The side of the valley nearer West and the local man was tree clad. Through the trees, a few small houses showed – all rather like the sharp edged white house of the Mallows. On a headland, a large, grey stone house stood with two turrets and castellated roofs. The land on the far side was mostly meadowland, cattle were grazing, ant like from here; and at the crest of one smooth, green breasted hill, a thick mass of white told of sheep in a pen.

Two villages were in sight, one with a Norman towered church, one with a slender grey spire.

Hoole itself was divided by a narrow river, which looked bright and glistening this morning. West saw the three bridges – one suspension and two arched. From here, the arched bridges looked very old. It was possible to see the criss cross of narrow streets; only on the outskirts, in the new town, was there any hint of town planning. There were two parks, bright green and pleasant, and a dozen churches.

Wortleberry pointed.

"Not just sight seeing," he said, apologetically. "There's the London Road, road you came on, sixty one miles to Marble Arch from there. See. There's the road to the west, and there's the Worthing and Brighton Road. The main road, West, is about a mile away from us, but if you follow this one right round, past the cottage, you come out to it. Favourite walk, this, in the summer. Crowded on Sundays. There've been a lot of offers to buy it for building, but old Lord Hoole won't have it. He's chief landowner, Chief Constable, everything. He presented it to the town in trust, but now the trouble is that he hasn't got enough capital left to help us keep it up. Have to sell to the builders one of these days, I suppose, if we can't get some help from the National Trust. Sacrilege to build up here, though."

West nodded.

"Only house within miles is Reedon's cottage, and he fell on his feet when he got that," the local man went on. "It's just outside the Hoole property, falling to rack and ruin when he bought it. Used it just for weekends, for a year or so. Then he spent a bit of money, put in an electric light plant, and came here to live."

"Where from?"

"London, as far as I know," Wortleberry said. "Anyway, the place is worth a small fortune, now."

"Wonder where he got his money from," West said, almost idly. "Well, let's have a look round."

A few yards farther on, the cottage came in sight. It was timbered on the outside as well as in, the tiles were weathered red and covered with lichen. The windows were tiny, although one showed signs that it had been made larger recently; the surround looked new. There were three chimney stacks, and the rooms must be very low; the whole building hardly seemed high enough for two floors.

"People walk up here just to see the garden, in the spring," Wortleberry said. "Bit late now, but then it's a mass of rock flowers. Aubrietia, violets, wallflowers, tulips—oh, everything. Just a mass. His dwarf azaleas are a proper sight, too. Pity it's a between season."

West stopped the car and got out again. One glimpse told him that, between seasons or not, this garden was remarkable. The lay out of the rockery itself was beautifully done; there were streams, two pools, goldfish swimming lazily, tiny waterfalls; all in miniature, but none of it looking artificial. Here was a labour of love.

"Did Reedon do all this himself?" asked West.

"Oh, yes. Worshipped the place. Had a man in a few days a week for the vegetable garden at the back, though, and sold most of the vegetables, made quite a good thing out of it. Tomatoes, too. The garage is round the back, just an old barn; he wouldn't have anything that looked out of place. Car's still there." Wortleberry grumbled deep in his throat. "If I'd had my way I'd have been in here early, but the Chief says no, wait a bit, check the laundry marks on his clothes. Nothing in the pockets to help, you know. I'll certainly be surprised if the body we took out of the sea this morning isn't Reedon's. I've seen that bit nicked out of his right ear often enough, and I don't believe in that kind of coincidence. Going in back way or front way?"

"Let's try the front," West said.

They approached slowly, looking about them. The cottage with its long, crooked path, looked idyllic; very different from the battered body now lying on a bench in the autopsy room next to the police station. The garden looked as if it were one which someone loved.

The newspaper was still in the letterbox.

They tried the iron handle, and pushed the thick oak door; it wouldn't budge. Wortleberry took out a bunch of keys, selected a long, shiny skeleton one and, without a word, slid it into the lock and twisted and turned.

The big lock turned with a sharp click.

"Quick work," West said, and pushed the door when Wortleberry stepped aside for him. "Thanks."

He had to lower his head to get into the lounge beyond; standing upright, he would bump his head on the oak beam which stretched from above the fireplace to the opposite wall. Dark oak beams were flush with the other walls. The cottage had all the picturesque charm of a show place, and although it seemed dark after the bright sunlight, one could see well enough. Brasses and copper pieces gleamed on the walls, over the high mantelpiece, in the huge fireplace, with its gate and spits, its hanging hook, and the huge wrought iron dogs. Two muskets, crossed, were above the fireplace; there were other old pistols and matchlocks; a museum of old arms.

West wasn't thinking of the museum pieces.

He sniffed.

Wortleberry kept grumbling, in that perpetual way of his, and appeared to notice nothing.

West sniffed again, and then shuddered; nausea pulled at his stomach. He moved back, and opened the door wide.

By then Wortleberry also knew that something was amiss, but didn't appear to know what. Had he no sense of smell?

West said: "There it is, over there."

He pulled a white handkerchief from his pocket and put it to his nose, then led the way. Puzzled, Wortleberry kept close.

He wasn't puzzled for long.

The body of a man lay on the stone flagged floor of the kitchen. He had been dead for several days. And the cottage was not free from rats.

Chapter Five

Two Dead Men

West still went forward, but Wortleberry didn't. He stood still, head lowered because of the beams; and his ruddy face had lost colour. West, closer to the body, saw that there would be little difficulty in identification; the features were recognisable on one side of the face. The man had fair hair, turning grey, and looked young middle aged. The back of his head had been smashed in, and probably the first blows had killed him.

He wore a light grey suit, brown shoes, red socks, and an old raincoat. On the shoulders there was a white powdering, like flour. One of his knees was bent. He lay on his back, one arm across his chest, the other straight by his side. His head was turned towards the kitchen stove, enabling West to see what he had seen.

The hands had suffered most. West moved quickly, and made sure that the finger tips weren't destroyed.

He didn't linger, but went across to the two small kitchen windows, and opened them. Without a word, he and Wortleberry did the same thing in a small wash house, in the front room, and in a tiny study. In there was a fairly modern oak desk, a portable typewriter with its black cover on, papers, books, all the impedimenta of an office. It was scrupulously tidy, and probably the one room in the house where a telephone would not look out of place.

"Shall I send for—everything?" Wortleberry's face was quite expressionless now.

"As soon as you like."

Wortleberry took out a handkerchief, covered the telephone with it, then lifted it; he wasn't going to miss a trick, and he would be on his mettle with a Yard man here. West heard him give the police station number, ask for Inspector Porth, grumble noisily, and then tell the Inspector to come up to the cottage, bringing everything he would need for a murder probe.

"Yes, the body's here," Wortleberry said, "ambulance, doctor, photographers—well, everyone. Hurry." He paused, then said, "Goo'bye," and rang off.

West was bending over the body again, lips set tightly, head averted; he went through the pockets, brought out a few oddments, and put them aside.

Wortleberry went to move them.

There was nothing to name the dead man; money, keys, a comb, everything a man would usually carry – except papers which might help to identify him.

Wortleberry placed everything neatly on a table.

"Better have a look round upstairs," West said briskly.

They went out, and each man glanced at the body.

"Not Reedon?" West asked.

"Oh, no, Reedon's a younger man, and dark haired. That chap's forty five, shouldn't put Reedon more than thirty two or three. Bigger than that fellow, too."

They were close to the feet, and the narrow, twisting stairs led from the little passageway between the front room and the kitchen. West led the way up, Wortleberry's shoulders brushed the wall on either side.

Both men ducked big beams.

In the rooms both had to crouch, except in the main bedroom. They stopped to take a good look at everything, and photographed it on their minds. The hole in the ceiling, the chippings of plaster and the powder on the floor, thick just beneath the hole, but only a film on the rest of the uneven boards, on the bed panels, and the dressing table; it was on everything with a dark surface. Even the window ledges had a film of white dust, which had all come from the hole in the ceiling.

A chair was beneath the hole, as if a man had stood on it while making the hole or looking through it. The dead man's shoulders had a similar dusting of white.

"Take a dekko," Wortleberry said; without realising it, he whispered. "See what you can. Better not risk my weight on that chair."

It was an old William and Mary, with a slung leather seat and a slung leather back, worn almost black and very shiny. The legs were sturdy but of unequal thickness. It creaked as West got up on it, cautiously, took a slim torch from his pocket, and then looked into the loft, shining the torch round.

The beam fell upon a small packet. He could not see what it was at first. He fished it nearer, using the torch, and then saw the green design of one pound notes. He took the packet by one corner, held it gingerly, then pulled it out of the hole. As he did so, he pictured Daphne Mallow and the slimmer bundle of one pound notes. This one held two hundred and fifty at least; hers hadn't been anything like so thick.

"Found anything?" Wortleberry breathed.

"Yes," West said. He lowered himself out of the hole cautiously, then brought his hand down. "Don't want to smear any prints, although I shouldn't think there's much there." The Hoole man promptly unfolded a clean white handkerchief, and West put the wad on that, before climbing down. "Two hundred and fifty, I'd say. Oldish notes." His voice was low pitched, too. "I wonder exactly what we're up against."

The Superintendent was looking at the bundle. It was covered with dust, which stirred gently, and showed up vividly where a shaft of sunlight came into the room. Keeping it together was a strip of yellow gummed paper, stuck down to form a tight band; so the wad was slightly thicker at the ends, where there was no pressure, than in the middle, where it was constricted.

"I just don't know what we're up against," Wortleberry said very emphatically. "But I know that if Reedon had any more of that up there, it was probably—" Wortleberry stopped abruptly.

"There was plenty more, I could see where it stood," West said. "Perhaps he wasn't *left* any money, after all."

"If Reedon was a crook—" Wortleberry began, and then growled: "What's the matter with me, gassing like this? We've got a killer to find."

"One who crept behind that chap downstairs and smashed his head in—probably after he'd collected the money in the ceiling," West said. "We want cash and a killer."

"Wonder if Reedon and Mallow did this together, and skipped," Wortleberry said. He drew the corners of the handkerchief across the bundle of notes, then tied a neat knot. "My chaps won't be long. I usually leave it to them after a few general instructions, but if you want anything special done, just tell them."

"Thanks," said West.

Wortleberry frowned.

"Didn't you say that Mrs. Mallow had a bundle of notes in her hand? One pounds?"

"Yes. We'll have another talk with her as soon as we know if Mallow's really gone north. She had a worry all right, and I'd like to know what it was."

"Tell you something," Wortleberry announced, abruptly. "Mallow was always hard up. Borrowed money all round. Borrowed plenty from Reedon, too, but Reedon wasn't the only one. Nice chap, Michael Mallow, if it weren't for playing the fool in more ways than one."

He looked at the dead man again.

An hour later, Roger West left the cottage and walked to his car. The sun made it glisten, and the inside was very hot; he had forgotten to leave a window open. He got in, ignoring the dozen people who had reached the cottage, and were standing and staring. The ambulance, big and white, was still there, backed against the gate; the dead man would soon be carried into it. Three police cars and a small van had also arrived. Two uniformed policemen were on duty, one at the front gate and one at the back door, to make sure that no one forced entry. The people who had been passing by, or else heard a rumour, caught occasional glimpses of big men passing to and fro at the cottage windows.

They saw the flashes, when photographs were taken.

They didn't see the white chalk line which had been drawn round the body, or the thorough, painstaking search which Wortleberry was leading. The quest for finger prints, for anything which might give help, would go on long into the afternoon.

West started his engine.

People stared at him.

He drove off, going slowly, and in spite of the pressure of events, stopped when he reached the spot, near Demon's Cove, and looked over Hoole again. The sun was in exactly the right place, now; down in the town shadows looked sharp and black, the grey stone houses comparatively light, all the colours of roofs and walls were heightened.

He didn't stay for long, but drove down into the town, keeping to the tarred road.

The discovery of the body on the rocks, and the first rough description, had brought him post haste to Hoole, looking for the killer of two schoolgirls. There were several similarities between the body at Hoole and the wanted man. West – "Handsome" at the Yard – had driven down with a sanguine detective sergeant, Bradding, who had a relation at Hoole, and was now with the relation. The dead man he'd seen might be Reedon, but certainly wasn't the child killer.

Wortleberry had been anxious for him to stay until they knew more about the man.

"You've been in it from the beginning, seems crazy if you have to go back now," he had said, just before they had started for Mallow's cottage. "The Chief won't object, if you can fix it with the Yard. Will you try?"

Roger West was about to try.

He had a lot on his mind; not least, the recollection of his first realisation that something was seriously wrong at the cottage. He wouldn't forget the sight or the smell for a long time. It was the second corpse he'd seen in a few hours, but the first had hardly affected him.

The first lay on the bench; unless the autopsy had been finished, and it was back in the morgue.

West didn't go straight to the police station, but to the Old Ship Hotel, not far away from it, where he and Wortleberry were to have lunch. From outside, the hotel was ugly and bare; inside, one had a sense of promised comfort and good food. An elderly porter showed him the telephone booths. He called the Yard, and was lucky: the Assistant Commissioner was in.

The A.C. listened.

He probably grinned.

"I know what you mean, you'd like a nice little holiday by the seaside," he said, gruff and apparently aggressive. "Well, stay today, anyway. Don't upset Lord Hoole, he isn't the easiest of Chief Constables as it is. Let me know in the morning if you think it's worth staying longer. And have a drink at the Old Ship for me."

"What'll you have, sir?"

Chatworth chuckled.

That was a good sign, West reflected as he rang off. The "what'll you have" hadn't been flippant, but had been asked so as to test the A.C.'s mood. He didn't really feel sore, or suspect that West had seen a chance of taking it easy for a day or two.

Chatworth got queer ideas, sometimes.

Now the ball was in Wortleberry's hands. The local man felt sure that he could "manage" the Chief Constable; probably by the middle of the afternoon West would be here officially.

One man, dead in the sea, with his skull smashed in.

One man, dead in the cottage, with his skull smashed in.

At least one inescapable piece of material evidence; the bundle of notes, pointing to a possible motive for Reedon's murder – but had he been killed or was he the killer? It was too early to speculate about the second murder.

Mrs. Mallow's nervousness; her fears; her eagerness to hide the one pound notes; her sudden onslaught of dread when he'd let her know that Reedon might have been the victim of violence. Michael Mallow, a friend of Reedon's, known to be short of money, and away for a long weekend, which Wortleberry had said was unusual.

One of the biggest enemies of the police was lost time.

West didn't leave the box, but put in another call to the Yard, and this time asked for Detective Inspector Turnbull.

"Having a nice time, Handsome?" The voice from London was deep, and the tone half mocking.

"Just up your street. Two bodies." West said. "I want you to find out what you can about a Michael Mallow, a traveller for Mildmay's, the office equipment people. Thirty ish, fair haired, good looking, blue eyes, weighs about twelve stone. He lives down here at Hoole. He's supposed to be on a job in Scotland, but I doubt it. There's an inquiry in from Hoole already—but this is a special for me. If he's not in Scotland on company business, I'll get a photograph."

"Right. Any idea what it's about?"

"Just work on that, will you?"

"Okay," said Turnbull. "Have a good sleep." He rang off.

Roger went briskly across to the police station, and arrived almost at the same time as Wortleberry, who stepped like a carelessly made giant, almost more freak than man, up the police station steps.

"Tell you one thing," he rumbled, as they reached the shadowy main hall. "I'm having Daphne Mallow watched. Sorry, she's a nice kid, but that money's got under my skin. Sure she did have pound notes?"

"Positive."

"What I want is an excuse to get a search warrant," Wortleberry said. "Any ideas?"

"Just let her know she's being watched, and see if it worries her," West said. "And find out whether her husband has really been away since last Monday, or whether she was lying about that. If she lied, and I think she did, it was about the husband."

"I've got a feeling," Wortleberry announced solemnly. "When we have a chat with Mallow, we'll learn more than we know so far. I've a good chap watching his wife, anyhow." He turned into his office. "We'll have a wash over at the Old Ship. Gor! I'm famished."

"Anything in about that bicycle?" West asked.

"Eh? Don't you ever *feel* hungry?" Wortleberry sorted papers. "Ah. Just a routine report—sand on the tyres from the top of the cliff, Mrs. M.'s prints—they assume so, we'll check—and that's about all."

"No other prints?"

"A man's. No reason why a man shouldn't ride his wife's bike."

"No," agreed West, and grinned. "Well—check with neighbours if Mallow's been seen this weekend, on the bike or in his car. Check if car—"

"It's all being done," Wortleberry said. "Come'n eat."

Chapter Six

The Watcher

Daphne Mallow looked out of the window, at five o'clock that afternoon, and saw the man.

She had never seen a man standing along the road, like this, until today. He was doing nothing. He was tall, lean, and rather ugly, wearing a pale brown suit and a hat with a big brim.

The watcher kept looking towards the house.

Twice in the past two hours, he had left the spot where he stood most of the time, and had walked right round White Villa. He'd just strolled casually, and Daphne had caught sight of him among the trees at the end of the garden, hands in pocket, cigarette in his mouth. He hadn't said a word, and hadn't been nearer than fifty yards away from her at any time; yet the sight and the thought of him caused that fear to rise again, like a smouldering fire blazing up. When he was out of sight, she felt as if he was able to see through the walls of the house into the room.

First, Michael's fear and flight.

Then the waiting.

Then, suddenly, the two policemen, including one from Scotland Yard, and the way the Yard man had looked at and questioned her, and left her with her heart pounding with inexplicable fears because of the implication about Tony.

Now, the watching man.

She was not positive that he was a policeman, although she felt sure.

She felt – suffocated.

Every window in White Villa was open as wide as it could go. The scent of the flowers, the smells of the grass and of the countryside, came in with all their richness, and should have soothed her; instead, every little sound scared her. The angry hissing of a bluebottle, swooping about and then smacking against the window, was enough to make her jump. The flight of a bird across the window would make her spring to her feet. She did not know that it was the accumulation of fear; that her nerves had started to go to pieces on the morning when she had woken to see Michael packing. That had been a shock, and she'd had no chance to recover from it.

She wanted to scream: *"Where is he?"*

She wanted to talk to someone whom she knew; her mother, perhaps, or Tony, but she daren't go away, she had to wait here to find out what happened next.

Where was Tony?

She sat close to the window in a small armchair, with some knitting in her hands; she was only making a pretence of knitting. The wool and the half made garment were soft white, to feed the hope which she always had for a child. She gave that no thought, now. Whenever she looked up, she could see the man.

He moved.

Her heart began to beat fast, and she started to get up, then dropped back into her chair.

The man was coming nearer.

She heard the sound of a car engine, not far off, and immediately she thought of the police, not of Michael. It seemed as if Michael had walked out of her life when he had gone out to the garage.

The man slouched past the house, looking in at her, making sure that she knew that he was watching; and then, while she tried not to stare, the telephone bell rang. She swung round, with a sudden flurry. She knew that it might be anyone, a friend, a tradesman – *Michael*. She jumped to her feet and darted across the room, standing at first with her back to the window, as she snatched up the receiver.

"Hallo! Mrs. Mallow here."

"Is that Mrs. Michael Mallow?"

It wasn't Michael. She felt as if her knees would collapse under her. She leaned against the wall, and that way, was sideways to the window.

"Yes," she said, in a husky voice.

"Good afternoon, Mrs. Mallow," said the man, in a brisk voice. "This is the *Daily Comet*. I'm sorry to worry you on such a matter, but I would be grateful if you could give me a little information about the late Mr. Anthony Reedon. I understand that he was a close friend of Mr. Mallow's."

She didn't answer.

She was hearing just one phrase over and over again. "… the late Mr. Anthony Reedon." She felt herself quivering. Then she saw a movement in the garden, and gasped, turned her head, and saw the tall man walking towards the front door.

"Are you there, Mrs. Mallow?" the *Daily Comet* man demanded.

"I—I don't understand you," Daphne gasped. "Mr. Reedon—Mr. Reedon can't be dead. I don't believe—"

She stopped, knowing that she wasn't making sense; realising that a London newspaper would not make a mistake. *The late Mr. Anthony Reedon.* "I'm sorry," she said chokily; not really knowing what she was saying. "I can't stop now. Goodbye."

She put the receiver down.

The front door bell rang.

She stood near the telephone for several seconds, and then some hard core of strength came to her rescue, and she straightened up and moved towards the hall. She must not behave like this. She must get a grip on herself. She must talk to someone; Mother, of course. She felt better when she opened the door, although she didn't feel well. She was simply determined to put up a better show.

"Good afternoon."

"Good afternoon, Mrs. Mallow." It was the watcher. He had a Sussex burr and a soft voice, and somehow couldn't make himself look anything less than friendly as he stared at her. The sinister, watching figure just became a man. "Is Mr. Mallow home yet?"

That attacked her new resolve, but she fended it off.

"No, I'm sorry, he isn't."

"Has he telephoned?"

"No," she said; and the feeling of suffocation grew worse.

"You haven't heard from him?"

"*No!*" The moment she shouted, she wished she hadn't. The friendly eyes of the tall man in front of her looked just a little embarrassed, and yet he gave the impression that he was satisfied. "No, I—I'm sorry. I mean, why do you want to know? Who are you?"

"I'm Detective Officer Bradding, Mrs. Mallow." The caller took a card from his outer breast pocket so quickly that it was like sleight of hand. He thrust it in front of her, but didn't seem to expect her to take it. She glanced down. It was too close to her eyes, and she had to back away a little. All she read were the words: *New Scotland Yard.* "Do you think Mr. Mallow will be back tonight?" the tall man asked.

"I—no. Well, I don't know. I—"

"If he comes, telephone the police station at once, won't you?" asked Bradding. "It's very important."

"*Why?*" she breathed.

He looked really sorry for her. He stood with his hat in his hand, and his head held back, his grey eyes narrowed and his broad face set in a funny kind of half smile.

"A personal matter," he said. "Sorry to worry you, Mrs. Mallow." He made to put his hat on again, and then lowered it: "When did he last see Mr. Anthony Reedon, do you know?"

She didn't answer. She wanted to turn away from him, go in, slam the door in that smooth face with its false friendliness. Yet she knew that if she did, it would be folly. The shock of that *"the late Mr. Anthony Reedon"* still lay harshly upon her.

"I—I've told the others, it—it was a week last Thursday. We went up to have a drink. We—" She was clutching the door, actually hurting her fingers. She stopped, and then blurted out the question which tormented her. "Is it—is it true that Mr. Reedon's dead?"

"Oh, yes," answered Detective Sergeant Bradding, in his slow voice. "There is a suspicion of foul play."

Daphne's grip on the door was very tight for a moment that followed; it was as if the door was her only means of support; if she let it go, she would collapse. Every muscle and every nerve in her body seemed to go tight, and to hurt. Her teeth clamped against each other, her lips felt rigid.

Suddenly, she went limp.

Bradding saw what was happening, stepped forward, and slid an arm round her. She fell against it. He had to hold her tightly, to keep her up; she was a very pretty, very shapely woman, in a dead faint.

Bradding gave a funny kind of shrug.

He put his other arm beneath her knees, lifted her bodily, and carried her into the bright red and white room, with its small recesses and flowers growing on the walls. A long, crimson couch was drawn diagonally across the French window, overlooking the big back garden. He laid her on this, and stuffed a cream coloured cushion beneath her dark head. He unzipped her skirt, then the girdle beneath it, and moved away quickly.

Her pulse wasn't bad. If he left her, she might be out for one minute; or for five, and come to no harm.

In two minutes, he had opened every drawer in this room, and found nothing he wanted. The unconscious woman hadn't moved, and he couldn't hear her breathing. He slipped out of here into the small dining room, where there was a writing bureau in fumed oak; the furniture and *décor* were as modern as the other.

There were books that might be worth a study, but the thing he was looking for was a wad of pound notes. He saw the letter from Netherby at Mildmay's London office, skimmed it through, and made a mental note of the address.

He passed the drawing room door on his way to the kitchen, listened, and heard nothing. The kitchen was a house wife's dream; there wasn't any hint of a smell of frying or cooking, of fruit, spices, or vegetables.

On the glass fronted cupboard which served as a dresser was a large, red handbag. How the woman loved red! Bradding opened it quickly, and looked inside. Nothing was there. He hunted round, peering behind packages and tins.

He found the wad of notes behind some sugar.

Bradding left White Villa twenty minutes later, full of apologies, telling Daphne to get in touch with the police if she felt worried. Looking round at her from the garden gate was like looking at a ghost. She was closing the door. Bradding didn't stay there long, but hurried towards the end of the road. Another man, who hadn't been in evidence before, moved out of the shadow of some trees to speak to him.

"How is she?"

"In a bad way. Watch her closely."

"Right," the second man said. "No one's certain that Mallow was in the car that left Saturday morning—several people heard it, but that's all."

"Can't be helped," Bradding said.

He didn't say anything about the letter from Netherby, and all it implied.

Bradding walked another hundred yards, and then went to a parked car. Two minutes later, he was on the way to Hoole. Twenty minutes later still, he was in Superintendent Wortleberry's room, where Roger West was already officially installed at a borrowed desk, with telephone, typewriter, and everything he needed except elbow room.

Bradding reported, and added: "I took some specimen numbers, so that we can get some idea when the notes were issued, sir."

He handed over a slip of paper.

"Fine," West said, and looked at Wortleberry. "So if he went to Scotland, it wasn't for Mildmay's. If you can spare a man, we'd better have his wife watched all the time, night and day. Avoid letting her know it from now on. We'd better have her telephone fixed, and listen in. If she posts a letter, get it before it leaves Hoole—can you fix that with your postmaster?"

Wortleberry said: "No, but I can fix it."

West found himself warming to the ungainly man.

"Fine! We just want to stop any letters addressed to her, and see what's inside them. Then check on the relationship between her and Reedon. If Mallow is the killer, it might have been for the money, or it might have been jealousy. Anything is guesswork at this stage." He knew that sounded prosy. "Then we want a call out for Michael Mallow."

"Any publicity yet?" asked Bradding.

"Better keep it in the family for the time being. We need to check on Mallow's movements, his work, whether he's in more serious trouble than a few hundred pounds worth of debts and a couple of tenuous girl friends." West paused, and added unexpectedly: "His wife's in for a rough time. The quicker it's over, the better for her, as well as the rest of us."

The other two nodded.

Daphne watched the tall man reach the front garden gate, and then turned away. She closed the door with a snap, but didn't notice it. Her head ached dreadfully, and she felt parched. She had insisted on getting up from the couch, but as she made her way towards it, she staggered; she felt that if she could reach it again and stretch out her legs she would stay there for an age.

It was very quiet.

She could remember the smiling face of the man from Scotland Yard, with his local dialect and soft voice and his smooth manner. She felt no hatred towards him; just a dread of things she did not understand. But she could put two and two together. Michael's flight, and the police interest in him, and Tony's – *murder?*

She shivered, uncontrollably.

The detective had put a glass of water on a small table near the couch. She picked it up and sipped. Cigarettes were near, too; she lit one, but it tasted harsh and unpleasant on her dry mouth, and she soon stubbed it out.

She longed for a cup of tea.

She got up, ten minutes after Bradding had gone, and went slowly into the kitchen. She felt as if she were in a curiously unreal world, as if all these familiar things were a long way off, and not really hers.

Mechanically, she put on a kettle, then set a tray for tea, took a biscuit tin out of the glazed dresser, and then stood looking over the stainless steel sink into the back garden. Lawns, flower beds, a few fruit trees, the little woods at the back. She did most of the gardening, Michael only bent his back to it now and again, without enthusiasm. The lawn wanted cutting; that was something she could do.

The kettle began to boil.

She spun round. *Tony was dead, perhaps murdered: Michael had run away.*

She could scream. She was standing here and thinking about the *grass* when terror was so close.

She made tea.

She decided to take it into the drawing room; she would be more comfortable there. Since the faint, her legs and arms felt weak, as if she had undergone some great strain, and was exhausted. She was half way towards the room, seeing the slanting sun striking one of the red chairs and making it a blazing crimson, when the telephone bell rang again.

She started; tea pot, cup, saucer, biscuit tin, spoon, sugar, and milk jug, all bounced on the tray. A trickle of tea came out of the spout, and a splash of milk appeared, bluish on the green glass surface. She quickened her pace. The bell rang again and again with long and urgent calls. She put the tray down, on a chair. Then she stood looking at the telephone, telling herself that it might be the police; or another newspaper; or a curious neighbour; and telling herself that she couldn't talk about it to anyone, now.

She lifted the telephone, slowly.

"This is—Mrs. Mallow."

A girl's voice came, clear and impersonal.

"Is that Hoole 1254?"

"Yes."

"Hold on, please, I have a long distance call for you."

The girl went away, and the line seemed to go dead; but nothing else was silent. Daphne's heart began that heavy, wild pounding, it was like the continual thudding of a dynamo inside her.

A long distance call.

Michael? Could it be?

Please, God, let it be Michael.

"Are you there, caller?" the impersonal voice said again. "Press button A, please, you're through."

"Please God—"

"Daff," said Michael, in a wonderful moment of time, "Daff, are you there? It's me, Mike. *Are you there?*"

Chapter Seven

Follow My Lady

Daphne heard his voice, knew that she had to answer, yet couldn't find words. She was choked, as if by some physical grip on her throat. But it wasn't physical; it was the suffocating hold of her nerves. She tried to speak, but could only make her lips quiver.

It did not last for long, but in it, Michael said hoarsely: "Daff, is that you? *Daff!*"

Because she was so sensitive to fear, she recognised it in his voice; there was something in the way he kept it low, in its hoarse urgency, which told her so.

"Yes," she managed to say in a strangled voice. "Mike, where are—?"

"I mustn't stay a minute," Michael said. "Have—have you been questioned?"

"I—yes," she said chokily.

"Are *they* still there?"

"Not—not in the house," she managed to say. "There's one outside, he—" She broke off. "Oh, Mike!" All her despair was in that cry.

"Listen to what I say, *carefully*," Michael urged. "I must have some money. Get as much as you can, and bring it to London tonight. I must have it tonight. I—I've got to go away. How much—how much do you think you can get?"

His voice, coming out of the earpiece, was saying these frightening things, and was as hoarse as if he hadn't had anything to drink for days; the kind of hoarseness that only comes from a parched throat.

"Mike, what happened? Tell—"

"How much can you get?" he screeched: and then swiftly, cringingly, went on: "I'll tell you everything when you get here, but I didn't do it, Daff. I swear I didn't."

"Did you know—?" she began.

"Don't keep arguing! How much can you bring?"

The answer came quite suddenly. She had that money behind the sugar tin, and she'd counted it twice; there were fifty one pounds. She had another ten or so, upstairs; she always kept a little reserve. She could cash a cheque at the Old Ship hotel, where she knew the manager, or one of her shops, if they weren't closed.

"About a hundred pounds," she said.

He seemed to gasp.

"A hundred? Wonderful, Daff. Listen, you know your passport? Bring it, will you? Never mind mine, mine won't be any good, but yours hasn't been altered since we were married, has it?"

"No."

"Bring it. Catch the six thirty. Go straight to Trafalgar Square, and wait by the lion opposite the National Gallery." Now his words came very quickly, almost glibly, and he wasn't so hoarse. "Tell you everything when you get here."

"Mike!" she cried. "Mr. Netherby—"

"Oh, to hell with Netherby!"

He rang off.

She couldn't believe it, but kept the receiver to her ear, and kept calling his name; loudly at first, then more quietly, then in a forlorn little whisper as she lowered the receiver slowly. She turned away. She forgot the tea, the couch, and her weakness. She remembered one thing he had said, and clung to it: "I didn't do it, Daff. I swear I didn't." But whatever he had or had not done, he was frightened; and was planning to flee the country.

Her clear, direct mind made a ruthless comment: that didn't sound like a man who'd committed no crime.

She went into the kitchen. The clock, in the shape of a frying pan of brightly polished steel hanging over the electric cooker, told her that it was nearly half past five. She had less than forty minutes in which to get ready, because it was a quarter of an hour's drive to the station. She would need a taxi, too. She would have to take some of her clothes and some of his. And the money.

There wouldn't be time to cash a cheque.

That made her heart drop; she'd promised him a hundred pounds, and he'd been delighted; in fact, it wouldn't be much more than sixty. Somehow, she felt that she had let him down. It nagged at her. Only the need to pack some things into a suitcase, to telephone for a taxi, to get everything else done, stopped her from brooding. She thought of the detective, Bradding, and the fact that he had gone; thank heavens he wasn't still watching.

She telephoned for a taxi; an elderly owner driver who served this part of Hoole was free. Then she had a brainwave.

"Mr. Micklem!" She shouted the name, fearing he'd gone.

"Yes, ma'am?"

"Mr. Micklem, I have to go to London in a hurry, and it's too late for the banks. I wonder if you could cash me a—a rather substantial cheque?"

He hesitated. Perhaps she shouldn't have asked him; anything that ate up time was a bad thing. She wanted to bang the receiver down, but had to wait for his deliberate reply.

"Well, I don't know about substantial," he said, "I don't reckon to keep much in the house, ma'am. I could manage fifteen pounds, if that's any good."

"Oh, that's wonderful! Thank you so much. Don't be late, will you, I must catch the train." She rang off.

By temperament she was calm, and by habit, tidy. And the crisis, added to the stimulus of having heard from Michael, cleared her mind. She knew that she wasn't feeling normal, that she might suddenly break down, as after a sleepless night; but for the moment she was right on top of everything. Her mind worked with great precision and clarity. By the time she reached their bedroom, which overlooked the front garden, she knew exactly what clothes she would take for them both; what case to use; what to say to Micklem. Her one fear was that she might be watched, but the tall man with that falsely friendly face had gone. Twice she looked out of the window, and saw no one.

What about the milk, newspapers, postman?

Micklem would stop the milk and newspapers for her, and the post could wait here. She wasn't likely to be away for very long. That thought conflicted with talk of leaving the country. The first moment she hesitated in that swift succession of incidents was when she opened the tin box where they kept their insurance policies, Post Office Savings Book, a little loose money, chequebooks, and the passports. She hesitated only for a moment before putting the Savings Book, chequebook, and her passport in her bag. She closed it with a snap. The pound notes were already there, except those from the housekeeping which she'd put under the paper which lined a dresser drawer.

At six o'clock she was putting on her hat. It wasn't likely to be cold, but she decided to take a heavy sweater, and one for Michael; he only took a raincoat round with him in the summer. She did all this without any thought of finality; without seriously thinking that she would be leaving the country, in flight. She was vague about everything that would happen once she got to London and saw Mike: that was the important thing.

If only she wasn't followed!

Micklem arrived in his antiquated black Austin, at five past six. Daphne was ready, with the case already in the hall. With his slow, deliberate courtesy, Micklem lifted his peaked cap off his bald head, wished her good evening, hoped that bad news was not taking her away so hurriedly. His old eyes, watery and grave, seemed to regard her with close attention.

She wished they hadn't.

She sat back in the comfortable old car as it rattled and squeaked over the bumps and the pot holes, looking right and left for the tall detective.

The only man she saw was one in a boiler suit, working at a telegraph fuse box in the road. He'd dug a biggish hole, and when the taxi passed, straightened up to wipe his forehead with a brawny forearm. Then he squatted down by the hole again, and went on with his work, apparently not interested in Daphne.

Roger West was at the telephone in the big office, alone for the first time that afternoon. He held on for a call, not yet knowing who was making it. It had just turned six, and the office caught the evening sun. His coat was off, shirtsleeves rolled up, tie loose; he felt as much at home as if he were in his own office. His one regret was that he had to telephone his wife, and tell her that he wouldn't be home. After fifteen years of marriage, she would still be acutely disappointed.

A man spoke: "Chief Inspector West?"

"Speaking."

"Osborn here, sir, the man who's been watching Mrs. Mallow's place. Thought you ought to know that the taxi's just called there, and the driver's walking back to his cab carrying a suitcase."

West said: "Nice work, thanks. What's the cab make and number?"

Osborn told him.

"Thanks again," West said, and rang off.

He had been told about Daphne Mallow's talk with Micklem, but the call from her husband had come just too soon for the man listening at the telephone.

Wortleberry came in. He listened, his dull eyes brightened, his small hands moved as he picked up a telephone and a pencil at the same time.

"Old black Austin, OK42M, Ted Micklem's usual cab, ta." He spoke into the telephone, almost in the same breath. "Have someone nip over to the station, Perce, if Ted Micklem's cab comes in with a passenger, ring me at once." He rang off; and not for the first time, surprised West with the speed with which he could move; he didn't look a hustler, and now it seemed as if he was making quite sure that he wasn't outpaced. "That confirms that she's catching the six thirty."

"To London?"

"Yes, Victoria."

"Any stops on the way?"

"Horsham, Guildford."

"Pity," said West, "that means someone ought to be on the train after her, it's no use having the train met. I ought to clear up a few oddments at my desk, and if there's a London end to this, my chaps'll have to be alerted. Will it upset your plans if I go to London, and come down again in the morning?"

Wortleberry snuffled and smiled.

"I was going to tell my wife to expect a visitor to supper, that's all. 'Nother time. So she's really going to join him," he added, and obviously he was thinking profoundly about Mallow's wife. "Can't blame her, I suppose. Look, I'd better come over with you, we can clear up the oddments on the way."

"Good idea," said West.

They hurried downstairs.

"Station's only five minutes' walk," Wortleberry said, "we should be there before the lady. I've just come from Dr. Samson, who did the autopsy, and he had Reedon's dentist there for a look at the teeth. No doubt the body we took out of the sea is Reedon's. I knew I wasn't wrong about that nick in the ear," Wortleberry added, with deep satisfaction. "So that's that. We've got nothing new on the other chap, though. Clothes off the peg at Burtley's, shoes from Wilson's, underwear and shirt all what you'd expect, and nothing much in his wallet. Coupla pounds. But his dabs are on the way to the Yard now, and a description, measurement, weight, and everything. If you know him up there, it might help a lot."

"I'll ring you tonight," West promised.

"Ta. Like to know," Wortleberry added. "He's not a local chap, anyway, that's one of the reasons why I'm glad you're on the job. I'll tell you what it looks like to me," added the local man, as they walked along crowded pavements across the one wide street in Hoole; the High Street at the Market Place. He lumbered along, and somehow no one got in his way. Somewhere not far off, a train hooted and whistled. People were queueing in hundreds for the long, single decker buses which served the outlying parts of the town and countryside. The day was still and warm, and the clinging smell of petrol was more noticeable to West than it had been all day; thick and offensive, too. "It looks like this," the local detective went on, guiding West towards a zebra crossing. "Over there. Anthony Reedon did a big job some time ago, and came to live here like a gentleman. Retired, sort of. This chap we found dead at the cottage knew about it, p'raps he didn't think he'd had a big enough cut, and came along and dug the cache out. Michael Mallow was in it with the second fellow, and they had a row."

They were across the road; fewer people were on the other side. The train whistled again, and there was a sudden hiss of escaping steam.

"Something like that," West agreed.

He marvelled that this big man, with the placid, routine mind, the thoroughness and the years of experience, would trot out a theory so glibly. To Wortleberry, probably, all things were simple. Well, this might be.

They turned up a narrow alley, and found themselves almost at the station; the carriage approach was from the other side, a long way round.

"We can watch the platform from the bridge," Wortleberry explained, "and when she gets into her carriage, you can decide which one you want. You know," he added almost gustily, "I've half a mind to come with you. You know what?"

"What?"

"Only time I've ever been to the Yard was on a kind of Cook's Tour!"

"Any time you feel like a busman's holiday," West said promptly, "you come round with me."

"I'll take you up on that," said Wortleberry. "Up there." He nodded to the wizened old ticket collector at a little barrier. "The gentleman's from Scotland Yard, Joe," he said. "Okay?"

"Sure, Sam. Pay on the train."

"Ta."

They went up narrow wooden steps, and then joined the main steps leading from one platform to the bridge which crossed the railway. Here was the smell of soot and smoke, fire and steam, which could only be associated with a railway station. The bridge was glass covered, and hot. The floor was wooden, and most people were hurrying. One train came fussing in, another stood at a platform marked in big white on pale green: 2.

"That's your train. See the entrance? She should be here any minute," Wortleberry added. "It's twenty two minutes past."

West didn't speak.

Less than a minute later, Daphne Mallow walked through the ticket barrier, carrying her own suitcase, a square, biscuit coloured one with bright red corners. Looking down, West saw how smoothly she moved, how nice she looked. "Nice" was the right word; any man expecting her to go eagerly to meet him, should think himself lucky. She hesitated before going into a third class carriage.

"When Mallow goes by train, it's always first," Wortleberry observed. "She's the careful one in that family."

"I'm just beginning to realise the value of living in a small town," West said warmly. "I wouldn't like to try to keep many secrets from you. How was Lord Hoole when you saw him this afternoon?"

"Sunny, for him. Apparently he's heard a lot about you, and said he wants to meet you."

"Tell him I'm going to ask for an interview tomorrow afternoon," said West, "and ask him if it's all right to search White Villa. On a warrant, of course! The Mallows might be back tomorrow, it could be our only easy chance. And if he'll give you the warrant, do the job yourself, won't you?"

"I will," Wortleberry rumbled. "In person."

They shook hands and then West hurried down the wide stairs leading to the train. He could get in a carriage behind the woman's without passing her window, so she wouldn't see him. It didn't occur to him that there was the remotest chance of danger; or any chance of failure. The girl wasn't a practised rogue, it was unlikely that she dreamed that she was being followed. The only risk was of losing her in the crowd at Victoria.

Roger watched the other passengers, keeping his usual sharp look out, but he didn't see a man who was coming out of the refreshment room, opposite the end of the train. The man started for the platform, saw him, stopped, and backed away hastily. The door slammed. The man moved, and watched West through a refreshment room window. West got into a first class compartment, one carriage removed from the end. He took the last remaining corner seat, wished he had a newspaper, looked out of the window and saw the man coming out of the refreshment room. The pale, rather nondescript face didn't mean a thing to him, and the man turned and walked towards the far end of the train. He was very shabby.

West took out cigarettes.

He'd keep up with the job, might make a quick arrest if he found Michael Mallow and the interview went the way it should, and then he could get home for the night. It wasn't often that everything worked out as smoothly. The minor irritation of having no newspaper was soon smoothed, for within ten minutes of starting off, a fellow passenger offered him one.

"Thanks very much," said Roger West, and stretched out his legs and prepared for a comfortable hour and a quarter's run.

The train ran into Victoria on the dot of seven forty five. Roger was first out of the compartment. A little crowd of people from the third class carriage behind followed him. He wasn't in a hurry, because he wanted to make sure that Daphne Mallow didn't catch sight of him. He saw her getting out. A fellow passenger, big, youngish, and with very red hair, handed her down her case, and then obviously offered to carry it for her. Her protest was ineffectual. West let them start for the ticket barrier, then followed thirty yards behind.

Mallow's wife had nice legs, and no wobble. She—

West felt his legs hooked from under him, and fell forward with frightening suddenness. He had no time to think of anything but the sudden collapse of his legs when something pushed his shoulder. He felt himself hurtling off the platform, on to the other line.

He heard the scream of a whistle, the rumble of a train.

Chapter Eight

The Yard Gets Busy

Roger West hadn't a chance to save himself.

He had been close to the edge, so as to get round the man; as he was pushed, he saw the glistening metals of the rails, the flints between the wooden sleepers, the sleepers themselves almost black with oil. He was falling head first. All he could do was bring up his arms to save his head, but banging his head wasn't the cause of dread.

The deafening whistle seemed just behind him, splitting his head in two.

Pheeeeeew!

Head cradled in his arms, he hit the track. Pain jolted through one elbow and shoulder. He sprawled on the rails. He heard the screaming whistle and felt the sleepers and the very ground itself trembling as the locomotive came hurtling towards him. What thoughts he had were fragments; it wouldn't come fast into the buffers, the driver must have seen him, he'd brake. But West knew better. He snatched his arms away from his head, and started to scramble to his feet, but it would take time; and the locomotive was almost on him, a massive monster of iron and steel, hissing steam, whistling, screeching, brakes squealing. He hadn't time to get to his feet. On his knees, he did a kind of scrambling run, then flung himself forward.

The noise was thunder in his ears. He waited for the impact, for the pain, for the crunch of his bones. He felt something very hot, close to his face, then the wind of the passing loco, then a completely new sensation: he hadn't been crushed, hadn't been touched.

His body flopped.

For a second he lay face downwards, not knowing that his feet were only inches from the wheels of the train which was drawing into the station. He fought for breath; shock itself was enough to kill, and he had never seen death come closer. Then, with sudden new alarm, he realised that a train might soon come in on this line. Spurred by that fear, he looked right and left, but the track was quite empty. It was a gleaming line of rails in one direction, with buildings a long way off; and the great roof of the station, the buffers of this line, and the platform in the other.

The train had stopped, and the only sound now was of the escaping steam.

He pulled himself to his feet.

This was an end platform, and no one was on it. The carriages and the locomotive hid people from the other platform. He stood up, and leaned against the edge of the platform, still breathing hard, arms folded, head limply on them. He hadn't yet the strength to climb up, but he was already feeling much better; so much so that he could worry about Daphne Mallow.

But not for long.

The long, empty line of the platform, broken only by a few wooden seats, advertisement hoardings, and several heavy crates obviously waiting for the next train, was suddenly disturbed. Men appeared at the far end, by the ticket barrier, and began to run; three appeared first, others followed until there was a crocodile of them, in double and single file; most were porters, although some were in ordinary clothes. West knew what they wanted, what drove them so fast: fear for him.

He took his arms off the edge of the platform, and waved. They didn't check their pace, but waved back, and in a few seconds they were hauling him up, saying they couldn't believe it, that he ought to be dead.

He had only one question in his mind, and put it swiftly: "Did you catch the man who did it?"

There was a sudden, complete cessation of the mutter of voices; all expressions of delight and relief ceased at once. The grimy men stared at him, and every face had the same kind of startled expression.

"No one did it," one of them said. "It was an accident."

Roger West sat at a desk in the station master's office, opposite the assistant station master in his navy blue uniform, gold braided cap, and dignity. Two clerks and one porter were also in the office. Roger had the telephone at his ear, and was tapping his toes impatiently on the floor. It was ten minutes since he had been hauled up; fifteen or more since the girl had escaped, and he still wasn't through to the Yard.

Then a girl said: "Scotland Yard, can I help you?"

"This is West—who's in the Chief Inspectors' room, now?"

"Mr. Cortland, sir."

"Put me through, please," Roger said. Cortland was a good chap, and he wouldn't lose any time. "Hallo, Corty, Handsome here. Have you seen anything about that Hoole job?"

"Just looking through it," Cortland said. "The local chap's sent a mass of stuff, including photographs of this man Mallow, his wife—"

"Mrs. Mallow?" Roger broke in eagerly.

"What's the matter with you?" asked Cortland. "Deaf?"

"Funny stuff later, please," Roger pleaded. Bless Wortleberry for sending that photograph! "That girl's in London. She arrived at Victoria at seven forty five. She had a big yellow case with red corners. We want her, just as soon as we can get her. She's probably meeting her husband, either or both of them will do. His car's a Vauxhall, blue, note up there about it already." He paused, and then went on much more slowly: "Don't hold her until she leads you to him."

"For Handsome West, you're nearly incoherent," Cortland said dryly. "Had some trouble?"

"I bumped my funny bone," Roger said. "Thanks, old chap. I'll be along soon." He rang off.

The assistant station master had a worried, wrinkled look, the two clerks were gaping, the only man who seemed to take this in his stride was the porter. He said emphatically that he had been close to West, and was sure that West had been pushed. No one else seemed to have seen that. The porter was short and young, with very wide shoulders and big hands and feet. He carried his peaked cap; a deep ridge on his forehead showed that it was a size too small.

"I can hardly believe—" the assistant station master began.

"I know, nor can I," Roger said, and grinned at the porter, proof that he felt much better. His elbow hurt a bit when he moved his arm, but that was nothing that massage and rest wouldn't put right, and it was his left arm. It wasn't pleasant to think about what might have happened, but he was in a hurry to get away from here. "Still, the chap tripped and pushed me. Do you mind getting your station police busy, and finding out if anyone else saw it?"

"I shall do that at once, of course, but—"

"Oh, 'e was pushed," asserted the porter, his Cockney accent so rich that it seemed affected. "The chap who did it was wearing a mack and a trilby, too. He just gave a side kick, and then bumped the gentleman wiv' his shoulder. It was all over in a tick."

"Did you see his face?" asked Roger.

"Never had a chance," the porter said, "but I can tell you one thing, guv'nor. He had holes in the soles of his boots."

"Boots?"

"That's right, old fashioned boots, all wrinkled," said the porter. "Down at heel and wiv' 'oles in the soles. 'Oles," he repeated, and an enormous grin spread slowly over his ugly face, "in his soles!"

"Like to come along to the Yard with me, and make a statement?" Roger asked briskly.

Blue eyes glowed. "Wouldn't I!" said the porter, with delight. "That's if it's okay with you, sir."

He looked at the assistant station master as if to say that this was one invitation that couldn't be overruled.

"Of course, of course," said the assistant station master.

There was something about Scotland Yard in the evening that it didn't have by day. A kind of expectancy; a feeling that anything might happen at any moment. The continual movement of the Squad cars was somehow more exciting than it was in broad daylight. The figures of men in the courtyard looked bigger. In the building itself, few of the clerical staff were on duty, but active C.I.D. men were on the move all the time. Every telephone call might be significant. The administrative offices were all closed, but the executive departments were kept busy: Ballistics, Finger prints, Records, Photography – these and a dozen others were fully manned. One could get any fact one wanted without delay. In an odd way, everything seemed to happen more quickly. The footsteps on the stone floors sounded louder, bells more shrill, voices held a note of suppressed excitement.

Roger left the porter, one Charles Sullivan, with a sergeant and a uniformed policeman in a waiting room, busy with his statement, and hurried up to the Chief Inspectors' Room, which he shared with four others. Cortland was still there. Roger's desk, one of the five painted and varnished a biliousy yellow, was in a corner by the window overlooking the Embankment. The window was open a few inches, and the noises off the river and from the Embankment came in. Big Ben, only a hundred yards away, boomed as the door opened. Instinctively, Roger looked at his watch; it was half past eight.

Cortland, a bulky man in a suit of grey so dark that it was almost black, raised a big hand.

"Funny bone all right?"

"The real damage was to the railway line I banged it on," Roger said mildly, and ignored Cortland's comical start of surprise. "Nothing in about the Mallows, I suppose?"

"Not a thing, except that Mallow didn't pick his wife up in their Vauxhall."

Roger's eyes sparkled.

"Found it?"

"On a parking site, Enfield way—been there a couple of days, almost out of juice. Don't ask me why it wasn't reported before, I'll have someone's skin. We've got it at the garage, now, giving it a going over."

"Might be a help." Roger didn't sound hopeful.

"We're checking the cabs, we should soon know who took the dame from Victoria," Cortland went on. "Did you say—?"

"Between ourselves, yes, but I lied. I don't like the chap who did it, though. Booted and down at heel with holes in his soles!" Cortland looked positively shaken. "Did you have any word from Finger prints about that chap we found in the cottage?"

"Haven't heard yet," Cortland said weakly.

"You probably would have if there's been any luck," said Roger almost glumly. He pulled out his chair and sat at his desk, looking through the mass of papers on a tray marked: *In* and another marked: *Pending*. He slid one or two sheafs of papers out, but left most of them where they were. "Sorry if I'm brusque, but beneath my bright facade I'm feeling sore." He lit a cigarette. "Have a look at the situation for me, will you, you're fresh to it. Reedon, now suspected of an old burglary, murdered and thrown into the sea. There's no doubt he was injured before he went into the water, the blows on the head were almost certainly caused by hand." Roger was still looking through the papers he'd sifted from the mass. "At his cottage, the second man was lying dead. Judging from the condition of his clothes, he'd obviously made a hole in the loft, where we found a bundle of one pound notes. There had been a lot of other bundles there, and a box with sharp corners – we found scratches; so, a metal box. Can't think why he left one bundle, unless he heard someone downstairs, and went down. The position of the body makes it possible that he was struck on the back of the head as he reached the foot of the stairs, and turned the wrong way – for him. He was killed by blows over the head, with a heavy article – could have been taken from the walls of the cottage. No trace of it, anyhow. It looks as if he lifted the hoard from the secret hiding place, and then a third man killed him and lifted it in turn."

"This Mallow?" asked Cortland.

"Dunno. Haven't found Mallow's prints there yet. Still, it looks that way." Roger went into more detail, and then finished his sorting. "I'm going to take this home with me, if I get home at all tonight," he said. But he didn't move. "Look at this angle, Corty, and tell me if I'm crazy. I followed Mallow's wife. Nice, simple job, I could have done it with one eye closed. She'd be conspicuous in any crowd. But someone also followed me. That someone presumably was on that train, had been at Hoole, had noticed and followed me, and meant to make sure that I didn't catch up with her, and so trace Mallow."

Cortland nodded his comprehension.

"Who'd want to follow her, who'd want to find Mallow, and why?"

Cortland scratched his big jaw.

"Supposing there were two chaps at the cottage, in the first place, one to do the job, the other to keep a look out. Supposing Mallow knew about one, dealt with him, and then went off with the boodle. The chap on look out would know he had it, and go after him. If he didn't know where Mallow had gone, he'd wait for his wife to make some move, and follow her. And if he's got a record he'd have recognised you, and wanted you out of the way." Cortland paused. "That what you're thinking?"

"Yes."

"Pity," said Cortland, with a grimace. "But you're not crazy yet."

Roger grinned.

"Thanks. So we've built up a nice theory, that someone is now after Mallow to get the money. Whoever it is didn't mind pushing me in front of a Kentish Special, so he won't mind a little violence."

Cortland said: "Oh," in a heavy way. "I see."

"I think I'll get along to Finger prints," Roger added, and jumped up on the words. "If Dalby brings in the porter who's making a statement, tell him to buy the chap a beer, and charge it to me, will you?"

Cortland said: "Okay, Handsome."

He watched with brooding eyes as Roger left.

He was a man with twenty five years' experience at the Yard, and was acutely sensitive to atmosphere. It wasn't exactly presentiment; it was more a kind of short cut, almost subconscious reasoning.

Given the circumstances which Handsome West had outlined, then more violence was not only a probability; it was almost certain if things went wrong with the bad men.

Cortland knew that West sensed and was probably oppressed by the risk. He also suspected that West saw some other factor he hadn't yet talked about; had seized on some piece of evidence which gave him a fresh slant.

The door closed.

Roger went quickly up to the next floor, and tapped at the closed door of Finger prints. The tap was cursory. The two men in sight, at a desk surrounded by tall shelving filled with files of papers, looked up. One went on with what he was doing, the other gave a broad grin. The night man in the Department, known as Fingers, had the roundest face of any man on the Force, and it was as red as a turkey's coxcomb.

He raised a hand, and made a circle, by putting his thumb and forefinger together.

"Hi!" he greeted.

"Hi," said Roger almost mechanically. "Sorry to see you're overworking. Had any luck with those prints sent up from Hoole?"

Fingers raised the other hand and did exactly the same thing. His grin was still very broad.

"Yes," he announced. "Just got round to it. You've got a nice job on your hands, you have."

Roger felt as if he had been kicked; felt his heart contract and then start to beat very fast. You could be a policeman all your life, and still have that happen.

"Who's the dead man?"

He could picture that body, with the bloodstains and the gnawed cheek and hands, the fingers hardly touched on the left hand.

"Chips Silver," Fingers announced. "Remember Chips? He got ten years for attempted murder, his luck was that the man he attacked didn't die. He didn't work alone, though, did he?" Fingers appeared to be enjoying himself; and Roger saw that and saw something else, which sent his pulse beat to a new high level. "He worked with Lefty

Ginn, and they don't come any worse than Lefty. You're after a killer all right, Handsome."

The evening seemed to chill.

He was after a killer.

And the killer had been after Daphne Mallow, at Victoria.

Not all the resources of the Yard could make sure that the woman was safe, if Lefty Ginn was after her. And Ginn would be, if he thought that she could lead him to her husband and what was left of the hoard of money.

The call went out at once: at all costs find Ginn. He hadn't been inside for many years, and nothing had been heard of him at the Yard lately; it was as if someone long dead had come to life again. Men on the Force who remembered him in his heyday had to think hard even to remember his friends and associates. There was no known address.

One or two whispers came in: that he had been seen at Camberwell lately; at the docks; that he had joined the Merchant Navy; that he was seldom in England. Roger West collected the scrappy reports, and tried to form a picture. No one at the Yard or at CB Division – in one of the most squalid parts of the East End, and near Ginn's old home – would admit for a moment that Ginn could have reformed.

"If he's out of one racket, it's because he's found another that pays off better," burly Superintendent Lumsden of CB said to Roger over the telephone.

"Sure he's not been around lately?"

"I'd know if he'd been within a mile."

"What about his family?"

"His wife left him years ago—after she'd shopped him for cruelty to their two children."

"Is she still living in your alley?"

"Well, yes, but—"

"We've got to try everything," Roger said. "Sorry, Lum. Have a word with her, or send one of your smarter chaps, will you? Ex-wives have a way of getting to know a lot about their formers."

"I'll try anything once, for you," Lumsden said.

Roger rang off. Other reports were coming in, and two were unexpected; that someone looking like Ginn had been seen near St. Paul's. St. Paul's wasn't reckoned to be a district for the Ginns of London, even after the great fire of 1941 had laid waste so many acres. Yet the reports came in quick succession; one from a sergeant once in CB now stationed in Holborn; he'd seen Ginn, and reported it, a note was on the station records.

It was.

Within ten minutes, a third report came in from a policeman usually on duty near the steps of St. Paul's. He was young, keen, and had a memory that would probably take him a long way. He'd never seen Ginn, only a ten year old photograph. Roger hadn't seen him, either, and didn't even remember seeing a photograph – he had just heard of Ginn's reputation. But the St. Paul's duty man was sure that on two or three occasions lately, usually just before dusk, he had seen a man answering Ginn's description passing St. Paul's, as if he was heading for Holborn across the devastated land.

"We'll concentrate the search there," Roger said. He detailed a sergeant to have two Squad cars sent to the St. Paul's area, and then lifted the telephone as it rang sharply. "West here."

"You're the luckiest copper in London." That was Lumsden's deep voice, and he sounded only half in jest. "I've had a word with Mrs. Ginn that was, Handsome, Mrs. Flannery that is. She saw Ginn only a week ago, in one of his old haunts down by the river. She says she isn't sure, but she thinks that he's got himself a nice, regular lady friend. Name of Gladys."

"Just Gladys?"

"I've only been on the job ten minutes!" Lumsden boomed protestingly.

"Like me to come and lend a hand?" Roger suggested; as he was speaking on the telephone, he didn't need to keep a straight face.

"I'll see you dead first! Ring you if anything else turns up."

There was a lull; in it, Roger had time to start worrying again, to feel bitterly angry with himself. There had been just that moment of almost carefree satisfaction, when it had seemed as if everything was going right; *right*. Then he'd stepped off the train, Daphne Mallow had been helped down by the big, red haired man, and – disaster.

He ought to go home; he ought to telephone his wife that he would be late. There were a thousand and one things he ought to do, and none so important as finding Daphne Mallow. That was now a personal responsibility—

Brrrrr-brrrrr!

"West speaking."

"Detective Inspector Mortimer here, sir, AB Division." The man had a rather thin voice. "I've just heard about the call for Lefty Ginn, I may be able to help."

Roger's hopes leapt.

"Fine. Go on."

"As a matter of fact, sir, I noticed him in the Division a few months ago, must have come off a ship. I've known he's been in the Merchant Navy for a long time, away for long stretches, usually. But this time he seemed to have settled down. He had a skirt with him—a girl, sir, she—"

"I know the vernacular."

"Yes, sir. She's younger than Ginn is. Twenty five or so. Name of Gladys Domwell. He stays at her place sometimes, where she lives with a married sister. Can't say I've seen anything suspicious, and I don't believe in keeping at a man if he's trying to go straight."

Roger said mechanically: "Quite right. Where's this married sister live?"

"At Number 111 Waterhouse Street, sir—that's between the Whitechapel Road and the river."

"I know," said Roger. "Ask your Super if he minds if you meet me there—half an hour, say."

"Oh, he won't, sir."

"Make sure, will you?" Roger said, and rang off.

More than enough trouble was caused by treading on the toes of Divisional seniors.

He felt an easing in the pressure; the line on Ginn had developed so quickly that they might find him before long.

Gladys Domwell's sister was a woman of nearly forty; big, heavy, mind and body tired out by a long family, a brutish husband, and a life of struggle. She looked jaded, faded, and worn when Roger saw her; and she talked the same way. Yes, her sister had two rooms in the house. Sometimes Lefty Ginn stayed, sometimes he didn't. More often, he didn't. He wasn't often there for more than a few days, and was often away for weeks. She didn't know where he went, and she didn't care – but yes, he was said to be at sea.

She didn't approve or disapprove of her sister's liaison. It wasn't her business. Glad was twenty six, old enough to know what she wanted, and to do what she liked. Glad paid on the nail every week, when Ginn was at home, he paid also. He didn't seem to be doing very well, though. She wasn't sure he'd had any work for a long time. If he wanted to know, she thought that he was out of work most of the time, and Glad was supporting him, but it was none of her business.

"What does your sister do for a living?" Roger asked.

The slattern drew herself up, as if she was trying to regain a little of the pride she had once had. She would have had good eyes, if she hadn't been so worn out; in her youth she had probably been wickedly attractive.

"She's as honest as *you* are, mister. Works at Riddle's, the glove maker's in Whitechapel – why, she brings work home, sunnines! Go and take a dekko in 'er room, if you want to."

That was exactly what Roger wanted.

He found nothing to help, as far as he could judge. Ginn kept a spare shirt, socks, and a spare pair of trousers here; these were old and threadbare, evidence that he wasn't doing very well. He had practically no belongings, which suggested that he probably had another "home" somewhere else. The slattern didn't know; or if she did, wouldn't admit it. She was insistent about her sister's industry and honesty, and there, in a tiny front bedroom, was a small glove making outfit, leather, cloth for lining, threads, glove moulds, stretchers – everything needed for home glove making. Gladys Domwell's clothes, if not expensive, weren't exactly cheap. For this district, she was doing very well; but would Ginn let himself be supported by a woman?

Roger tackled Gladys Domwell's sister again.

No, she didn't know whether Glad had gone to meet him tonight. He hadn't been here for a week or more. She could not tell the police anything else.

Roger left, haunted by the thought of Daphne Mallow with Ginn. Something in the little, smelly house, in the sordidness of the district, in the half frightened manner of the slattern, told him what it was easy not to realise: the real viciousness of Ginn. It had been brought home vividly.

Roger arranged for a special watch on the house, and to be called in person if Ginn or Gladys Domwell turned up, and went back to the Yard.

Nothing else had come in; and in his present mood no news was bad news.

Chapter Nine

The Lion

Daphne Mallow did not know that anything unusual had happened behind her, as she walked with the red haired young man towards the ticket barrier. She wished she was alone. The red head was Ben Norris, an acquaintance of Michael's, and they occasionally played tennis together. He'd talked too much on the way up, but at least he'd helped in one way: for he had talked of the body washed up on the beach, and told her the story of Anthony Reedon.

And he had told her of the body of an unknown man found at the cottage.

He hadn't noticed the panic in her eyes when she had learned of this. She had stared out of the window, at the passing countryside, so quiet and green, with the trees showing dark against the skyline, the wheat beginning to wave. She had gone absolutely rigid, as when the telephone bell had rung; but Ben Norris had a trait which served her well then.

Provided he was talking, he didn't mind what his listener did. She had only to make brief acknowledgments of his rhetorical questions, and look at him occasionally when she had recovered from the news of the second murder.

Now, he shortened his step to match hers, although she was striding out as best she could. He was still talking. Could they share a taxi? He was going across to Waterloo, but would gladly take her almost anywhere, he wasn't in any hurry.

"No," she said finally, "I'd rather not. Thank you all the same, Ben."

"Just as you like," Ben Norris said, "let me get a cab for you, anyhow."

"*No!*"

That pierced the smug blanket of his satisfaction with himself, but did no more than surprise him.

"Oh. Oh, well, okay. Well, it's been nice having a chat! Have to come and have a drink at the club one evening, when Michael's back." He gave a roguish grin. "Don't let him stay away for too many weekends, though."

She got rid of him.

She had noticed someone running, and someone shouting; and had overheard a man say that someone had fallen in front of a train. It meant nothing to her, but it helped, because Ben Norris obviously wanted to find out more; it was easy to smile brightly into his dull face, thank him, and hurry off.

She did not notice the man who followed her; who took a taxi after her; and whose taxi pulled up at the corner of St. Martin-in-the-Fields, the great church with its many steps and its huge pillars making a massive oasis of the past in that field of stone. She stood close to the railings of the National Gallery, the suitcase on the pavement, and stared across at the big lion, with its Sphinx like face, which the passing thousands ignored. The nearer fountain was playing, and water splashed noisily and was continually overflowing the big basin into the reservoir below. Crowds of people were farther away, feeding the pigeons. Above her head, the starlings roosting on the window ledges and the corners of the gallery, were singing their shrill, defiant song. The pale blue sky was crystal clear. Nelson lorded it over the lions, the fountains, and the people who had forgotten he was there, few of whom knew the real meaning of Trafalgar, except as a line and a date in a book.

Michael wasn't in sight, and she'd better cross the road. She had expected to be able to see from there, but couldn't.

He wasn't there, so at least she hadn't kept him waiting.

The suitcase was so heavy that she wished she'd left it at the cloakroom at Victoria; Ben Norris had made her forget. She felt so much more conspicuous, carrying it. A lot of men eyed her, and she could almost read their thoughts, it wouldn't be long before one asked if she would like some help.

She had never been more anxious to manage for herself.

She gripped the case firmly, waited until the traffic was brought to a stop by the lights, and then, with fifty or sixty others, surged across the road. Her case knocked against a man's leg and a girl's knee; the look the girl gave her was a tale of the agony of laddered nylons. She flushed. The crowd sorted itself on the other side, some going one way, some another; she was almost alone with the case as at last she approached the big lion.

Pigeons strutted on the pavement, picking at some crumbs left there and forgotten. A boy and a girl came hurrying, met, kissed, hugged, and went off hand in hand. Daphne looked in all directions, but still couldn't see Michael.

Why wasn't he here?

A youngish man with fair hair came hurrying across the road, only his hair showing at first. Daphne moved forward, eagerly, only to see a complete stranger.

She did not really notice anyone else, and the man who sidled up to her, after she had been there three or four minutes, took her completely by surprise. His voice came from her side; she just hadn't noticed him. It was a clipped, hard voice, and when she looked into the flabby, unshaven face, she saw hardness, too. Cruelty?

"You Mrs. Michael Mallow?" he asked.

"Yes!" she exclaimed. "Have you—?"

She stopped, in sudden horror. This might be a detective. She might have undone everything in that one crazy "yes". She stared with eyes which were suddenly bright with fear into the pale face.

"I'm a friend of his," the man said.

She didn't believe it; but at least she felt reasonably sure that he wasn't a policeman. He was too short, for one thing; she was taller by at least two inches. He was shabbily dressed, and badly needed a shave; a down at heel type altogether. Could Michael be friendly with—?

"He can't get here," the man said. "Wants you to come with me."

She began: "He can't—" and then let her voice trail off.

She stared into the cold, grey eyes of the shabby man. She didn't like the look of him, but he knew that she was to meet Michael here, so he might be telling the truth.

"It's not far," the shabby man said. "Let me take your case."

He didn't smile. She smelt strong, offensive tobacco on his breath. His hat was stained and very old, and his voice was almost like one which had been hardened like steel; it didn't grate, but wasn't really smooth or free.

He picked up the case.

"Why—why can't he get here?" She didn't want to go, but knew she would have to. "What's happened to him?"

"Nothing, lady," the man said. "He's doing all right. He daren't risk being seen, that's all. If you want to help him, better hurry."

What was there to do, but go with him?

He was already moving away, towards the National Gallery, and the one way road which led past it. The lion, the square, and everything on it were now behind her.

Michael was behind her, too, on the other side of the square, hurrying.

The shabby man stood by the kerb, still holding the suitcase, and watching traffic as it came surging towards them from traffic lights farther away and out of sight. He was looking for something; Daphne didn't know what. She saw his thin, almost colourless mouth, the lips pressed tightly together, and the hardness about his features and his skin. He was small but compact, and she thought that he was probably very strong.

He raised his hand suddenly, and whistled; the whistle was loud enough to startle her.

A taxi turned towards them.

"Inside," he said.

He opened the door before it stopped, and when she was inside, dropping on to the seat, he swung the suitcase in as if it was a handbag, and followed swiftly. The case had weighed her down. He sat on the edge of the seat, and glanced out of the window. Then he hitched himself forward, to speak to the driver.

"S'n Paul's," he said sharply. "I'm in a hurry."

He didn't move from the edge of his seat, but seemed to stay there deliberately. Yet he couldn't hide the Square from Daphne; she glimpsed part of it. She wasn't really looking for anything; the lion seemed to draw her gaze, and she moved her head to catch sight of it.

The taxi stopped, as the lights changed.

The man by her side shifted his position so that he blocked more of the window; then she knew that he was trying to stop her from seeing out. His face was very close. In the darkness of the old, box type taxi, it looked not only hard, but sinister; his eyes seemed to glint. She felt her breath coming in short, frightened gasps.

"Wha—?" she began.

The cab lurched, the man swayed, she was able to see out of the window, and was looking straight at the bronze lion.

Michael was there!

She opened her mouth to cry: "Michael!" but before she could, before she had time to be frightened of this man, to begin to understand the significance of what had happened, the man's hand closed harshly over her mouth. He pushed her back against the seat, snatched at her right wrist, and gripped it tightly. It was like being gripped by a steel spring.

"If you ever want to see him alive again, shut your mouth," the shabby man breathed. "Don't make any mistake. You could get yourself hurt if you're not careful."

The taxi was speeding towards the Strand, leaving the lion and Michael behind. The shabby man took his hand away from her mouth, but still held her wrist; and although he wasn't hurting, she knew that at the slightest whim, he could twist it and cause her agony.

"Do what I tell you, and you'll both be okay," he said.

He didn't let her go.

She didn't cry out, but only stared, too overcome by the new fears to think.

Michael Mallow did not see his wife getting into the taxi. The fountain and the lion hid her and the shabby man from sight. Staring at the spot where he had told Daphne to meet him, he did in fact see the taxi passing, and the shoulder, neck, and the shabby hat of the man who was blocking the window. That was all. He stopped, a yard away from the lion, and looked about him. A clock in a corner building, by the Strand, said ten past eight; anyone who caught the six thirty from Hoole ought to be here by eight o'clock, or just after.

He had tried to time his arrival perfectly, so as to avoid waiting, and so making himself conspicuous; he hadn't dreamed she would be late, or suspected for a moment that she wouldn't wait.

He stood still, with the traffic swirling, crowds of people making sudden surges across the road, while the huge red buses, the large and the small cars and the lorries and vans waited with snarling impatience, and seemed to shout as they leapt forward whenever a light turned green.

Mallow wore a light raincoat, in spite of the warmth of the evening, and it made him look conspicuous; many men were in their shirt sleeves, some carrying coats over their arms. His hair was almost too fair; usually it stood up like a mop of fine wire, but now it was forcibly flattened with water and brilliantine. His good looking face was set in lines of anxiety which took the handsomeness away. Strain showed at the corners of his full lips, at his blue eyes. He couldn't keep his eyes still. A cigarette at his lips was drooping a little, and there was a pale brown stain on his upper lip, from the nicotine of a dozen cigarettes smoked in the past few hours.

He began to pace to and fro, scanning the Square and Whitehall. Once he started to walk towards Whitehall, but turned back, muttering.

He hadn't been away from the lion for two minutes, but when he got there, a girl was waiting.

It wasn't Daphne, or anyone remotely like Daphne. She had glossy black hair, worn in a page boy bob, and bold brown eyes and a figure which no one could sneeze at. She was made up more than most London girls, and that, as well as something in her manner, gave her a kind of boldness; she was almost brazen. She smiled at Mallow, a faint, sneery kind of smile, which nevertheless had invitation in it. He stared intently; it was his habit to stare at women, especially young women. He sensed something about this one which was different from many.

He turned abruptly, to look back at Whitehall. Daphne would be bound to come by taxi. Victoria Street first, then Parliament Square, into Parliament Street, along Whitehall – there was nothing to take a taxi more than ten minutes, and now it was almost half past eight.

He let the cigarette drop, trod it out, and lit another; the packet was almost empty.

"Waiting for someone?" the girl asked casually.

He looked round at her sharply, and his expression became aloof, disdainful.

"Not interested," he sneered.

Although he turned away, he caught the beginning of a broader smile on her painted lips. She didn't come much higher than his shoulder, but the slanting sun glistened on that beautiful, jet black hair; as black as Daphne's, and much thicker and more naturally wavy.

"You will be," she said.

He started, and swung round on her.

"What's that?"

"You will be," she repeated.

"Will be what?"

"Interested."

"What the hell are you talking about?"

"I'm just saying that you will be interested in me, Mike," she said. Her voice was throaty and not at all displeasing. "You're coming with me."

For a moment, he didn't speak, just stared as if the truth were dawning on him slowly. She seemed genuinely amused. Suddenly, she put an arm through his, and drew him towards her.

"Let's get away from here, it's too public," she said. "Your wife's gone ahead of us, she's with Lefty Ginn. Know Lefty?"

"I—no! Who—who is he?"

"You'll find out," she said.

Chapter Ten

Lefty Ginn

Lefty Ginn did not know whether he would succeed in getting away with Mallow's wife until they were actually out of the taxi and walking near St. Paul's Cathedral across the land which had been devastated, and was not yet built up. In the warm evening, with the sun shining across and casting the huge shadow of the great dome, Ginn walked with Daphne along a narrow street, with brick walls on either side, no higher than their waists.

Ginn kept a hold on Daphne's arm with his left hand; and carried her suitcase. It seemed to be as light, to him, as a bag of feathers. He walked briskly, and because she was being forced along, partly by her own fears and partly by the thrust of his arm, she went quickly. They were in step. The pavement on which they walked rang clearly to their footsteps.

Behind them was St. Paul's.

About them were the deep recesses in the ground, all brick or concrete walls of what had been cellars and basements of old office buildings and of shops which had once clustered about the churchyard as thickly as combs in a beehive. Then, the narrow streets with their smooth, tarred surfaces had been dark and crowded and pulsing with the life of the city; now, the cellars were open to the blue sky. Where rat and beetle, house spider and mouse had lurked furtively, birds now nested, bees hummed from wild flower to wild flower, and grass grew long, waving whenever there was a breeze. Here and there stood the skeletons of buildings, one of which had been only half demolished, and which was unsafe. It was towards one of these that Ginn led the girl. A few temporary buildings, squat, square, and ugly, stood amid the desolation. Here and there, too, flowers had been planted and gardens made.

Ginn did not quicken his pace; and Daphne couldn't free herself. She was frightened; only the thought of seeing and helping Michael kept her going.

Ginn knew that a number of people noticed them, but none was near enough to see the contrast between her smartness and his shabby, threadbare clothes. There was a line of buildings, not far from Holborn, a few floors of which were still serviceable; and beyond them, the ordinary buildings of the city which had escaped in the great fire. The noises of traffic came clearly, although it was from the City, not from the West End. Few people were about, and Ginn's sharp, hard eyes were watchful all the time.

He reached a high wall which had been shored up by heavy timbers. It led to a basement now open to the sky, with wild flowers and grass growing between cracks in the concrete base, and at the corners. In the shadow of the brooding wall, which had a sign painted in crimson, saying starkly, danger, was a flight of stone steps. Near this was an old boiler which had provided central heating.

"Down there," Ginn ordered.

For the first time, Daphne drew back.

"Where—where are you taking me?"

"He's hiding here," Ginn said. He didn't smile; he didn't look as if he would ever have much time for humour. "Go down."

"No! I want to see him. I—" She tried to free herself.

Ginn dropped the case, knocked her behind the knees with his right foot and, as she crumpled, lifted and carried her down the steps. He moved as easily as if he were carrying only her clothes, and so swiftly that she hardly realised what had happened.

When they were at the foot, he put her down, and said: "Stay there, and don't shout, or I'll cut your throat."

He went back for the suitcase.

The edges of the basement were a foot or more above her head; when there had been a floor above, there had been room to stand upright down here. There was no easy foothold, no way for her to climb up, and – *Michael* might be here. The one easy way up was by the steps. Ginn was angled against these for a moment, then against the sky. He leaned forward, snatched the case, and swung it over. Then he turned and ran down, his footsteps making the only sound. The world was silent and cut off, down here, and she had never been so afraid.

If she screamed—

His eyes frightened her.

"Come on," he said, and gripped her arm just above the elbow, urging her forward towards a corner.

She could see only the scorched brick, but there was more. He prised open a loose brick, then used a key; and part of the wall opened, as a door. Big steel hinges groaned and creaked. He held the door open with his foot, and thrust Daphne forward roughly, into a black void.

"*No!*" she cried.

But it was too late. He pushed her, and she went staggering. The floor was even and she did not fall, just steadied herself, her lips still parted but no cry coming now. The only light was from behind her, and that was being cut off. Ginn's shadow was cast, black and long, upon the floor; and then it was blacked out as the door closed and there was no light at all.

"Oh; please let me out of here," Daphne begged. "Let me out of here, please, *please.*"

He didn't answer. She heard a sound which she didn't understand. She dared not move. Then something scraped, and abruptly there was a blessed relief; light in this awful blackness. He had a petrol lighter with a big flame, all black and smoky at the top; the kind of light that ordinary petrol would give. He carried this to a candle stuck in a beer bottle, and the candle caught slowly. He let the cap fall on the lighter. The candle flame was very small, and grew smaller, until it looked as if it would go out. Then gradually it lengthened and the light grew bright.

She could see his face, with all the deceptive flabbiness, and the gimlet like eyes. She made herself look away from him, and saw the old mattress in a corner, the blankets which turned it into a bed, an upright chair, several boxes, and newspaper cuttings stuck to the wall, most of them pictures of girls in swim suits. Near the ceiling was a ventilation grid, with a piece of brown paper tacked over it, so that light couldn't show outside.

The door had a heavy iron lock, a big key, and several bolts. She didn't know that it had once been the basement vault of a bank, that the walls about it and the floor above were two feet thick, and as nearly soundproof as anything could be. The only risk of sound escaping was at the door.

In one corner was a cupboard; once a strong room within the vault.

"Sit down," Ginn ordered.

She didn't move.

"I don't want trouble with you," Ginn said flatly, "you don't matter to me, get that into your head. It's your husband I want, and the money he took from Reedon's place. But so long as you're here, do as you're told. I don't like having to tell anyone twice."

She backed to the chair, and sat down. She kept her knees very close together, although there was nothing personal in the way he looked at her. He tipped his battered hat on the back of his head, and took a small green packet of cigarettes from the pocket of his old raincoat. These were *Woodbines*. He lit a cigarette, put the packet back, but didn't blow out the smoke, either through his mouth or his nostrils; it was as if he absorbed it all as he breathed in.

"Now you're here, you stay here until I've got what I want," he said. "And that's all he's got." There was a brief pause; then: "Know where he's put the money?"

"No!"

"Sure?"

"Yes, I'm *sure*. I don't know anything about the money. I don't know what he's done!" She broke off, staring at the man who stood and watched her sceptically, with the cigarette smoking in the corner of his mouth, only slightly red at the tip. "I tell you I don't know! He telephoned me, said I was to meet him at—at Trafalgar Square."

"You'll meet him some other place, if he behaves himself," Ginn said coldly.

He moved towards her.

She cringed back, although he didn't raise a hand, did nothing to suggest that he was going to strike her. He didn't strike, but put a hand down and lifted the big handbag off her knees. He slid the long strap handle off her shoulder, and then walked away, nearer the candle. Sideways to her, he began to empty the bag; and every time he took something out, he glanced at her.

The candlelight flickered on his eyes.

Purse; compact; the envelope with the fifty one pounds in. He opened this, peered inside, and then slowly drew the money out. He flipped the wad against the heel of the thumb of his other hand, and for the first time a little, reluctant smile made his thin lips move. He put the bag down, and counted with the deliberation of a bank customer who doubted the cashier's accuracy. He uttered the numbers aloud, although only a whisper sounded in the strange sanctuary.

"Twenty seven, twenty eight, twenty nine ..."

"Forty nine, fifty, fifty one."

Now his lips were parted slightly; obviously he was deeply pleased. The candlelight shone on to his face when he turned to face Daphne. His mouth seemed empty of teeth; the mouth and the face were mask like, now, horribly unreal with the unreality of evil to a person who was mostly good.

"Where'd you get this from?"

"It—it was sent to me," Daphne gasped.

He didn't comment on that, but moved towards her, nipping the wad against the heel of his thumb; that made the only sound. He drew within a yard of her. He was still smiling, but with the candlelight behind him, his face was one dark shadow. Only his eyes glinted.

"Who sent it?"

"I don't know!"

"You're lying to me," Ginn said flatly; the smile vanished altogether, like a light being doused.

"Oh, I'm not," she cried, "it's the honest truth. It came by post, this morning, I don't know who sent it. Mike said he had to have some money, so I put it in my bag."

Something she said then didn't please him. In spite of the shadows, she saw his expression change. He stood motionless now, without flipping the notes or making any sound, just looking into her eyes. She thought she had known fear before; she had known nothing like this, nothing like the terror which seemed to turn her blood to water, to leave her limp and helpless and completely at this man's mercy.

"Say that again," he commanded.

"I don't know who sent it!" she sobbed.

"Say it *all* again."

"I don't know who sent it, that's the honest truth! It came by post, I don't know who sent it. Mike said he had to have some money, that's why I brought it."

She knew that she hadn't repeated the exact words, and she believed that he was trying to torment her, was only interested in making her suffer. She was surprised when he moved away; too surprised, at first, to be relieved. He began to flip the notes again.

"When did he say he had to have some money?"

"When he telephoned, this afternoon!"

"He say anything else?"

"No. I mean, not about the money, he was scared, he—he wanted me to bring my passport, he—" She couldn't go on.

He turned back to the handbag, and took out the rest of the contents. The only question he asked was about the other money; ten pounds in her purse, fifteen in an envelope which Micklem had given her. He seemed more satisfied. He seemed different, too, as if something had happened to make him think, and to make him brood.

Except for the money, he put everything back. He tucked the money into a dog eared wallet, and stuffed that into his coat pocket.

Then he took the cigarette from his lips; it had become just a blackened stub. He dropped it and trod it out.

"That's a start," he said, "but there's a lot more to come. When Mallow arrives, he's going to tell me where he put the rest of the dough, and why he can't get at it. He won't leave this place until he does; neither of you'll leave." Ginn's lips parted in that empty mouthed smile. "Be as good as a mausoleum, won't it?"

At the Yard, Roger West went through everything recorded about the case; it didn't amount to much. He paid most attention to a despatch which had been sent by special messenger from Hoole, with a brief covering note from Wortleberry. Most of it confirmed the results of Bradding's quick search of the house, and the fact that Daphne Mallow had fainted.

The gist of Netherby's letter was quoted, and Bradding had given the address of the London office of Mildmay's: 27 Butt Lane, Holborn. He'd better go himself, in the morning. He didn't like the idea of having to sit back and wait until morning for anything, but couldn't help himself. If Gladys Domwell didn't turn up, someone at Riddle's, the glove makers, might know where she was; even that was worth a visit.

He checked to make sure that everything was being done, and decided to go home. That presented a different kind of problem. He'd put off telephoning his wife, and she would be peeved; not seriously, but just enough to make it necessary to be in a good, resilient humour when he got back. He ought to have telephoned her. Now, he would have to steel himself to put up a show until her first phase of ill humour was over, and probably soon after that he would find himself telling her all about Daphne Mallow. His wife was the only person he knew who might have some idea of the personal responsibility he felt towards Daphne Mallow.

Chapter Eleven

Gladys

For the first few minutes after the girl had slid her arm through his, Michael Mallow didn't speak. He moved slowly, as if he hated the thought of going with her, but couldn't stop himself. Traffic lights hampered them; when they were about to cross, a cyclist beat the lights and drove them and a dozen others back on to the pavement. By the time the shouting and the indignant muttering was over, the lights had changed again. This time, the girl looked up at Mallow's face, and said tartly: "We're going to cross the road. Get it?"

He gulped, and nodded. They crossed the road, first to the National Gallery, then after a pause to the steps of St. Martin's. A stream of people was moving towards the bus stop at the far end of the iron railings about the massive church. A bus passed, and several people started to run for it; the girl didn't. She kept her arm in Mallow's.

"Where are we going?" he asked.

"For a bus ride."

"Are you taking me to see my wife?"

"Yes, but don't tell the world about it."

"Where is she?"

"I'll show you." They had reached the bus stop, and another bus drew alongside. She glanced up, said: "This is it," and gave him a little push.

He got in, and went inside. The bus was nearly empty. He dropped on to a seat near the entrance, and the girl sat beside him. She sat closer than she need, and slipped her hand into his, squeezing gently. Her shoulder and her leg pressed against him, too, and she looked at him with mingled pertness and mockery.

The conductor held out a hand.

"Fares, please."

Mallow put his hand to his trousers pocket, then gulped, avoided the conductor's eyes, and turned almost desperately to the girl.

"I—I didn't bring any money with me."

"Well, Mike, fancy that," she drawled, and took her hand away from his arm. She carried a small, shiny green handbag, opened it, and took out a shilling. "Two to St. Paul's," she said, and then very rapidly changed her mind. "No, two to The Bank!"

"Make up your mind," the conductor said.

"Say that again, and I'll give you a piece of mine," the girl said tartly.

The conductor stared; then winked. She smiled, quite free from malice. She had nice teeth and a nicely shaped mouth. Mallow noticed that as he noticed most things about women. She gave him the tickets, and said: "Gladys won't pay every time, honey."

"I—I'm sorry. Silly of me," he said. "Sorry." He settled back against the seat, then groped for her hand; she looked surprised, and all other expression left her face. He squeezed. "Glad, what's all this about?"

"Can't you guess?"

"No, I don't get it," he said, as if genuinely puzzled. "Where's Daff—Daphne," he amended quickly. "My wife."

"Gone for a little walk with Lefty," the girl said softly.

"Who is this Lefty?"

"Why don't you dry up? We don't want to tell all the bus," she said, and obviously she felt nervous. "You'll see soon enough, and if you do what you're told, everything will be hunky dorey. Just sit back, and relax."

Mallow moistened his lips, looked at her, stared for a moment at her glossy black hair, then stared out of the opposite window, at the passing crowd and the shops. They were passing the Strand Palace Hotel, where a commissionaire was talking to a newsboy. The bus was held up for a moment. The newsboy's handwritten placard said:

TWO SEASIDE MURDERS

Mallow glanced furtively at the girl, but the furtiveness served no purpose, she was looking at him, her shiny red lips twisted, the smile was nothing like so attractive now. He looked away. They started off again, stopped at Aldwych, and then swept on until they were outside the Law Courts. Here, the Strand and Fleet Street's narrow roadway were almost deserted, the long stretch of Fleet Street itself had only half a dozen cars in it, very few pedestrians, no policemen on duty. The bus was nearly empty, too. The tall, grey, stone buildings of the Law Courts were safe behind their locked and bolted gates. The bus started off smoothly.

Before it gained any speed, Mallow jumped up, pulled his hand away, stepped on to the platform and jumped off. He kept his balance easily enough, and stepped on to the pavement.

"*Here!*" cried the girl. She sprang to her feet, eyes blazing with indignation. The conductor began to grin. "Ring the bell, you grinning ape!" she spat at him, and searched for a bell push. She saw one, stabbed, then stood impatiently on the platform, staring back along the pale grey street. She couldn't see Mallow; could see very few people. She bit her glistening lips, and gripped the rail of the bus tightly. As soon as they slowed down, she started to get off.

"Take it easy," abjured the conductor, "you'll break your neck." He held her arm, firm with authority. The road was sliding swiftly by, it wouldn't have been safe to get off. The bus slowed down more, and he let her go. "Give him a kiss from me," he said brightly, and as she jumped off and glared round, he added with an infectious grin: "And don't pay his fare home if he ain't a good boy!"

She ignored the back chat, and hurried back towards the Law Courts. Her gaze, her expression, the very poise of her body, told of tension and strain and anxiety – the emotions which anyone who had failed Lefty Ginn might have. She didn't actually run, but was very close to it. A man turned out of an office building, missed a step, and watched her. She took no notice. He eyed her up and down as she passed, then shrugged and crossed the road.

She reached the Law Courts, and stared along Aldwych. Some way off, there were many more people. She stepped out smartly, but now she looked across to the other side of the Strand past the shell of St. Clement's Church. She saw no one with bright fair hair like Mallow. At a zebra crossing she hesitated, biting her lips and clenching her hands, because she didn't know what to do next. No one could hope to find a man in the crowds of the London streets. She moved away from the crossing, and went towards Kingsway, her gaze fixed on the road ahead, not on the doorways of the shops and offices on her right.

So she didn't see Mallow until he was close to her, catching up from behind.

"Going anywhere, Glad?" he asked.

She spun round, eyes rounded in startled relief. They were very fine eyes. He grinned at her, now, although he looked on edge. She didn't speak, but began to breathe heavily, as if she had been running for a long time. He took her arm, as masterfully as the conductor, and gave her a little squeeze.

"What the hell do you think you're doing?" she demanded, when she could breathe more evenly.

"Just doing it my way," he said cockily. "What's this all about, Glad? Where's my wife, and where were you taking me?"

"If you want to see her again—" she began.

They were walking towards Kingsway, and people were crowding on the other side of the road, although behind them were the nearly empty streets. Mallow changed his hold on Gladys's arm, and turned round; she had to turn with him. When they got back in step, Mallow was looking at her with a fierce kind of grin.

"What's it all about? Who's Lefty Ginn?"

"You'll find out soon enough."

"Not now, and not at any time, if I don't learn more about it all," Mallow said. "I'm not going where I'm told by anyone, even if she has got a nice pair of eyes and" – he grinned – "*and* pretty black hair. What's doing?"

She said: "Don't make any mistake about this, you mug. Lefty's got your wife. He followed her from Hoole, and when she went to Trafalgar Square, he was there to take her away. She didn't have a chance. I met them at Victoria, and then waited for you, we were pretty sure you two'd get together." Every word that Gladys uttered was in earnest, now; it was easy to see that she was driven by fear of what would happen if she failed in her mission. "Now we're going to see your wife and Lefty."

"What does Lefty want me for?"

"*Are* you dumb?" she snapped.

"Not so dumb as you seem to think," said Mallow sharply. "Give me an answer, Glad, I'm anxious to know."

"He wants the dough."

"What dough?"

"Listen," she said harshly, "what do you think I am?"

"I've been wondering," Mallow said. His voice was easy and his manner casual; he had changed remarkably since she had first met him. There was a nasty edge to his words, but that was all, except the look of tension which he fought back.

"So Lefty Ginn kidnapped—" He hesitated after the word, looking down at her with a touch of unbelief; then he went on: "—my wife, and you're to take me to them. If I hand over this dough you talk about, you'll let her go. Is that it?"

She nodded, slowly. Her gaze was very intent, as if she was trying to find out whether he was fooling her, and only pretending to be so innocent. She read nothing at all in his blue eyes. They were red rimmed and bloodshot, and the tautness of his lips remained. It was obvious that he was steeling himself to a great effort, was forcing himself to behave calmly.

"That's it," she said, "and Ginn's—a killer. He's on his uppers, and he's got to get some money." A new, pleading note crept into Gladys's voice. "Don't try to cheat Ginn. If you do—"

Something happened to Mallow. He sucked in his breath, gave a little gasping sound, gripped both her arms tightly, and said harshly:

"I cheat *him?* That's a good one! George, that's cool! He wants to get hold of money I haven't got, and talks about me cheating him!"

She tugged to free her arms.

"Let me go!"

"You go and tell Ginn that I wouldn't try to do a deal with a brute like that if I had the money," Mallow growled.

She got her hands free, and backed a pace.

"Listen, Mallow," she said breathlessly, "don't you understand plain English? He's got your wife. He's the kind who'd do anything to get his own way. You don't know what you're saying. If you don't turn up, he—" She broke off. "I tell you he's desperate. Everything's gone wrong for him lately, and—"

"This is one more thing that's gone wrong," Mallow said roughly, and pushed her away from him.

He turned and strode away.

She stood staring; and people, passing by, looked at her, saw the tense, scared expression on her face, and wondered what caused it. It was a long time before she turned round and went along Fleet Street, towards Ludgate Circus, the hill beyond, St. Paul's, and the ruins in the cathedral's shadow.

Now and again she looked back. She didn't see any sign of Mallow, but it was impossible to see in the shop doorways, or round the corner. Her feet dragged at first, but when she was near the Circus, she straightened her shoulders and began to walk more quickly, as if thinking that the sooner it was over, the better it would be.

Roger West said laughingly: "Now don't be a mutt, Scoop, there's plenty of time for you to decide what to do with your life. I didn't decide to be a policeman until I was twenty one! You're not eleven yet. Straighten out the furrowed brow, and let's have a laugh."

His elder son Martin, called Scoopy, looking nearer fifteen than his eleven years, screwed up his face, as if in dismay, and then gave a little snigger of a laugh, which came out in spite of himself. The younger Richard, watching all this, giggled almost nervously, and then announced: "*I'm* going to be a writer."

"You don't know what you're going to be," Scoopy said scornfully. "Well, Dad, some of the boys know what they're going to do when they're *nine.*"

"And I know what you're both going to do this minute," Janet West said. "Go to bed. And next time I tell you to be home at half past eight, don't go persuading Mrs. Lock or anyone else to telephone and say you'll be an hour late, or you won't go out for a week. Off with you."

"Oh, Mum—" they began in chorus.

"Boys," said Roger, in the voice which the years had taught them to obey.

"Okay," said Scoopy brightly. "Come on, Richard, you ought to have been in bed an hour ago. Didn't he, Mum?"

He put a large hand on Richard's shoulder, and the two boys went out. Before the door closed, there was a giggle; next, a scuffle.

"Oh, boys!" called Janet, "go and get your milk."

They went into the kitchen, and looked round the door a moment later. Richard, with milk round his mouth like smeared white lipstick.

"*Look* at your lips—" Janet began.

Richard started to wipe his lips with the back of his hand, caught his mother's eye and ducked out. Next moment they seemed to be throwing each other upstairs, but things quietened once they were there. They could be heard moving about from bedroom to bathroom with unusual sedateness.

"Hallo, darling," Roger said. "Tired?"

Janet West smiled, without much spirit.

"So-so," she agreed, "I've felt worse. But these *socks* get me down. It's never ending, if it isn't Scoop it's Richard, and if it isn't Richard it's—"

"Don't look at *me* like that!"

Janet, near exasperation, began to glare; but seeing Roger's broad grin, she relaxed and laughed. She pulled a box of wools and cottons towards her.

It was a quarter to ten.

Roger had been home for twenty minutes, arriving just before the boys. Janet had been in a near crotchety mood; she always disliked being left on her own unexpectedly, and as the boys grew older, she found herself relying on them more and more for company. At the same time she found herself forced into accepting the fact that Roger would often be out in the evening. But now all three of her "men" were home, the day was over, she could put her feet up on a pouffe and relax, even though she was drawing a grey stocking with an enormous hole over a blue darning mushroom which wasn't quite large enough to fill the hole.

Roger sat and looked at her; there were times when he would say, quite honestly, that it was his favourite form of recreation. He hadn't yet told her that he was likely to be called out again; that all the police of London, uniformed men and those in plain clothes, were on the look out for Lefty Ginn, Mallow, and Mallow's wife.

He kept trying to think if he'd overlooked anything. Once a call went out, as it had tonight, it was largely a matter of routine and luck; good luck meant that one of the men on duty would catch sight of a wanted man or woman, report, and have patrol or Squad cars on the spot quickly. Roger had hoped that there would be a message for him when he got home, but there'd been none.

His briefcase was by the side of his chair, unopened.

Janet, her mass of dark hair touched with grey, looked tired, but not so worn out as he had often known her. Sitting in a winged arm chair, her rose pink dress against bottle green moquette, a table lamp by her side making gossamer of her hair, she looked good; not beautiful, but just right. She had grey green eyes and a full mouth, and a figure that lacked nothing but wasn't obtrusive. She'd made up for Roger, but her nose was a little shiny.

The front room of their home in Bell Street, Chelsea, was pleasant and comfortable, with a lived in look. One or two pieces of furniture were beginning to get shabby. There were near threadbare patches in the carpet by the door and at the front of Roger's chair. But the baby grand piano looked as polished and new as when it had first been given to them on their wedding day; and the curtains were bright and fresh. Richard's battered school satchel hung over the back of a chair, and Martin's cap was on the floor by the door.

Janet asked suddenly: "Worried about a case?"

"I am, a bit," Roger admitted.

He hadn't told her about the train incident; with luck, it wouldn't get into the newspapers, and there was no need to alarm her; nothing suggested that it had been intended to injure him, only to stop him from following Daphne Mallow.

"That Hoole man?" Janet asked.

Roger had telephoned that morning to say where he was going.

"And matters arising." Roger picked up the briefcase, opened it, and took out a file. He handed Janet a photograph from the top of it; Daphne Mallow's. It was a recent one, and as studio portraits went, very good. "I was following her, and lost her at Victoria," Roger told Janet. "I fancy she was on the way to meet her husband. One or two really bad types are involved. It would be a nasty feeling if anything happened to her, after I'd let her slip through my fingers."

Janet was studying the photograph; she took her time over it, the sock mending forgotten. A bump upstairs broke the almost suspicious quiet.

"Yes," Janet said, "she looks very nice. Do you mean to say that her husband's a murderer?"

"Could be."

Janet handed him the picture back.

"It must be dreadful to be married to a man who does a thing like that," she said slowly. "Especially if you're in love with him." There was a pause; punctuated by three bumps upstairs. "Darling, pop up and tell them to get into bed."

"Right," Roger said, and got up.

Yes, it must be dreadful to be in love with a murderer. There wasn't yet any certainty that Mallow was a killer, but a lot of things were adding up. The most alarming was the intrusion of Ginn into the affair; it was sinister. Ginn had spent those seven years in prison for robbery with violence, but had kept out since. He'd been tried for murder, and been found not guilty, on a technicality which hadn't fooled anyone as to the real truth of his moral guilt. He was bad; the kind of bad man who would commit any crime, have no kind of scruple, have no kind of feeling; the kind of man who might kick a dog to death.

Roger went upstairs. One of the boys whispered something, and there was a loud creaking of bed springs, yet he didn't smile. He was wholly serious when he said he felt a personal sense of responsibility for Daphne Mallow. He couldn't think of anything left undone; the last thing he'd arranged, when at the Yard, was for a search to be made for Ginn's known friends – male and female. The outlook was poor. Mallow's wife had simply vanished, and the startling thing was that she had gone while carrying that conspicuous suitcase. But it was early yet; the call for her hadn't gone out until nearly half past eight; it was still daylight, and there was a good chance that someone would have spotted her, and report to the Yard or the nearest station.

The boys were in bed, sheets drawn up over their faces, only the tops of their heads showing; fun was fun, whether at seven years or eleven. Richard gave a smothered giggle. If Roger pulled the sheets down, he would probably find they hadn't got on their pyjamas. He toyed with the idea of snatching the sheets off – and the telephone bell rang.

As if worked by a press button, both boys turned the sheets down. Bright eyes glowed in bright pink faces.

"Telephone, Dad!"

"I've got ears, too," Roger said. He grinned. "Now no more nonsense, either of you, put the light out and get to sleep."

" 'Kay, Pop!" Richard was always the cheekiest.

"I say, Dad—" began Martin.

"Roger!" Janet called, in a sharp voice, "it's the Yard."

Her tone and the "Roger" couldn't have said more clearly that she wished the Yard to perdition; which meant that she had some cause to be afraid that he would be going out again.

"Coming!" He moved quickly. "Good night, boys. Mummy will be up in a minute, I expect."

He waved, hurried on to the small landing, and found Janet already near the top.

"Try not to go out again," she begged.

"I won't, if I can avoid it," he promised, but that was only partly true. He reached the telephone, hoping almost desperately that this would be news, that he would have to go off at once, to see Daphne Mallow, her husband, or Lefty Ginn. "West speaking," he said.

"Cortland here," said Cortland briskly. "They've picked Mallow up—or he picked himself up, one or the other. He's on his way to the Yard now. I've told a patrol car to call for you. Okay?"

"Fine, thanks," said Roger. "I'll be ready."

Chapter Twelve

The Cellar

Roger pushed open the door of the waiting room at the Yard, and saw Mallow jump. That was an indication of the state of his nerves. He was sitting in an old fashioned armchair by the window, which was open at the bottom; it looked out on to the inside courtyard, the Squad cars, and big, shadowy men always on the move. Now, it was dusk, and lights were springing up everywhere.

Mallow started to get up.

"Sit down," Roger said briskly. He didn't go farther in, but studied the man closely. The red rimmed, bloodshot, almost desperate eyes seemed to tell their own story; so did the drawn lines at the corners of the well shaped mouth. Mallow had a lean and hungry look, too. His hands drummed a nervous tattoo on the arms of the chair.

He hadn't yet been questioned, but had made a brief statement, saying that his wife had been kidnapped by some men he didn't know. Roger had picked the story up as he had come into the Yard, not losing a minute; the sergeant who'd told him was still outside, on his way back to his office. It was simple enough. A policeman on duty near Blackfriars Bridge had spotted Mallow, recognised him from a description passed on by a patrol sergeant, gone to speak to him – and been startled when Mallow had come forward jerkily.

"I'm Michael Mallow," he had said, "I want to see someone at the Yard, urgently, and haven't the price of my fare."

Ten minutes later, he'd arrived at the Yard, in a cab paid for by the policeman.

Roger saw the nervous quiver of his lips, and offered cigarettes. Mallow took one, and a light, with restrained eagerness; he drew the smoke in as if his life depended on it.

"Now what's all this about?" Roger asked. "I'm Chief Inspector West, in charge of the London end of the inquiry into Anthony Reedon's murder. Do you—?"

"I'm not here to talk about Tony Reedon or anyone else who might have been hurt down at Hoole," Mallow said roughly. "I—I've given myself up because I'm frightened for my wife. I've told you people twice already, when are you going to get something done?"

"You won't get better results by shouting," Roger said mildly. "Take it easy, Mr. Mallow. Every policeman in London's on the look out for your wife, she'll be found." He wished he felt sure. "What frightens you about her?"

Mallow drew at the cigarette; it burned nearly half way down its length.

"I was going to meet her at Trafalgar Square. I don't know how it happened, but someone else got there first, someone named Ginn. Lefty Ginn, I think the girl said. He took Daff off. The girl—the girl said something about him wanting money from me, he thinks I've got—I've got a fortune. I—I tried to follow the girl but lost her, and—"

Mallow broke off, jumped up, clenched his fists and shook them in Roger's face. *"Why the hell don't you try to find my wife?"*

The more excited he became, the calmer Roger had to be. And he had to get the facts right, too; had to try to see them in all their significance; and one thing, if it was a fact, was puzzling.

"What name do you say the girl gave?"

"Gladys. She—"

"I mean, what man did she name?"

"Then why the devil don't you say what you mean?" Mallow demanded. "Ginn, Lefty Ginn."

"Sure?"

"Of course I'm sure!"

"What did she say about him?"

Mallow hesitated, looked about to explode again, then made himself say: "She said he'd got Daphne. Said he wanted some money from me—she called it dough. D-o-u-g-h spells *dough!* And—" Mallow's lips tightened then he moistened them; and he looked truly afraid, his voice shrilled. "She said he was a killer, warned me not to—not to cross him." He paused again, but Roger let it ride. "She said he was on his uppers, desperate, and—a killer, don't you understand that? A *killer.*"

"Yes, I understood," Roger said flatly. "It's true, too."

"*What?*"

"If it's the Lefty Ginn we know, he is a killer."

Mallow stared at him for a long time; his eyes burned; his fists were clenched, his arms were by his sides. Then suddenly, hopelessly, he buried his face in his hands and sobbed: "Oh, God, what have I done, what have I done?"

Roger said, very gently: "Well, what have you done, Mallow? How did you get into all this? What happened to put your wife in danger from a man like Ginn?"

Mallow didn't answer, and didn't uncover his face.

"Until we know it all, we can't be sure of getting results. What have you done? Why should Ginn think—?"

Mallow lowered his hands, slowly. He looked very tired out and ill; as if he had a burning headache. His voice had lost its vigour, something seemed to have been drawn out of him.

"Nothing I can tell you," he said. "I know what you think, but it isn't true. I've told you what happened tonight, told you everything I can to help you find Daphne."

They eyed each other, in a kind of duel.

Roger was quite sure that Mallow could tell him much more; almost sure that he wouldn't, tonight. The issue couldn't be forced, there was no way of making the man talk if he didn't want to. Whatever he had done, apparently he had given himself up because of the threat to his wife; perhaps he felt an awful sense of guilt towards her.

"All right, but don't blame us if we can't find Ginn because of anything you've held back," Roger said suddenly. "This girl Gladys—what's she like?"

"What the devil does that—?" Mallow began, and then he broke off. "Oh, hell, I'm sorry. I feel as if I'm going mad. If anything happens to my wife because of me, I—" He broke off again, licked his lips, and said: "She said her name was Gladys. She's rather short, got long, dark hair, falls down nearly to her shoulders, brown eyes and—and, well, she's a ripe piece. Cushiony, you know. Got too much make up on. She had a yellow sweater and a brown skirt, I didn't notice her shoes. That's—that's all I can tell you."

Roger was already signalling to the detective officer who was taking notes.

"Get that description out, Harris, and make sure it's flashed to all patrol cars, all police stations, and all police boxes. Where did you lose her, Mr. Mallow?"

"Ludgate Circus way. A couple of buses hid her from me, she might have got on to one. I don't know. I hardly know whether I'm on my head or my heels. Get—get dizzy spells. I haven't eaten since lunch, I—I got scared."

"We'll get you a snack," Roger promised. The sergeant went out, and the door closed behind him. "Look here, Mr. Mallow," Roger went on, "you don't have to say anything, but I'm here alone, so nothing you say can be used as evidence. It can be used only if there's a witness. Hadn't you better get it all off your chest?"

Mallow's eyes were glittering, as if his head ached dreadfully.

"All I want is to make sure my wife's all right. I haven't got anything to say, apart from that. Except—*I* didn't kill Tony Reedon. It's crazy to think I did, he was my closest friend! I didn't kill him, understand. I'm not a murderer."

His voice rose, and his lips were quivering.

The officer came back, folding his notebook to another page. Mallow glanced at him, and then back to Roger; he'd finished the cigarette, and was looking round helplessly for an ash tray.

"Throw it in the grate," Roger said. "And sit down, Mr. Mallow. I've told you that you're under no obligation to make a statement, but I think you'd be wise to. In any case, I must ask you certain questions, and—"

"Why don't you go and look for my wife?" cried Mallow. "Find her first, I'll answer the questions afterwards. Oh, God, if anything happens to Daff I'll kill myself."

Roger said stonily: "Every possible effort is being made to find her, and if there's any need for me to join the search, I'll go at once. Meanwhile, it's time you answered questions. Were you in Hoole on the night of Friday, June 5th?"

Mallow set his lips, and refused to answer.

Fifteen minutes later, word came that a girl answering Gladys's description had been seen near St. Paul's; and within five minutes of that, another statement came from a policeman who had just seen the description of Daphne Mallow and the suitcase.

"With a short man wearing a mackintosh, north of St. Paul's," Roger said briskly. "Better have the whole of the flattened area cordoned off, and get the men who know the district best ready to start combing it. They may have gone through to Holborn, but if they did, why were they walking?"

He left Mallow at the Yard, on a nominal charge of having had stolen property in his keeping at his house at Hoole.

It was nearly dark when Roger reached the ruined part of London just behind St. Paul's. The lights of the distant main streets looked bright from here. In the distance, too, the smaller lights of cars and buses looked like a succession of fireflies moving in line. Closer at hand, police cars were clustered wherever there was an open space, men with torches were ready to start a search of the area. Roger was with a sergeant who knew the whole of the derelict area as well as he knew his own street. This was Sergeant Parker, of the uniformed branch.

The two men who'd reported Gladys and the other couple were standing by.

"If they all went along what used to be Kimble Lane, sir," the sergeant said, "they'd be heading for those buildings over there." He pointed. "See, there are two lights in the windows. Can't think of anywhere else they'd be going, not from what used to be Kimble Lane."

"We'll close round on that, then. What lies that way?"

"Well, it's about as bare as any part just here, sir," the sergeant said. "Lot of walls, three or four feet high. Lot of basements, too. The ground's like a great big honeycomb. Wouldn't be the first time we've found down-and-outs kipping—I mean sleeping—there, sir. Why, there was a man and woman living there right under our noses, actually rigged up electric light from a meter next door, *and* running water. Always slipped in when it was dark, see, they were all right until they got too bold and started using their 'flat' by day." Sergeant Parker was wondrously solemn. "Proper rabbit warren, sir. And no one much ever goes to have a look round there—except we policemen, but we can't see through brick walls." That wasn't near insolence, but a stolid statement of fact. "Not far away from here we found that little girl, last year. Ugly job, that was."

Roger thought of the case which had sent him to Hoole, and would harass him until it was solved.

"Yes," he said. "If you wanted a hide out, where would you have it?"

"Oh, over there, sir." Without hesitation, Parker pointed towards the direction in which the wanted trio had been seen; and towards the cellar where Ginn and the girl were in hiding. "But be careful near that big wall with the red light on, sir. Dangerous, that is—scheduled to be knocked down next week."

"We'll be careful," Roger promised.

"So he wouldn't come," Ginn said, "and you let him go, did you?"

He'd said it half a dozen times, as if it was the only thing he could think of. He hadn't done anything yet; hadn't touched Gladys, or threatened her. Now, he stood by the box which had the candle on it, looking at Gladys, apparently oblivious of the fact that Daphne Mallow was here.

Gladys answered as she had each time: "I couldn't *carry* him, could I?"

"You couldn't have made him understand."

"Of course I made him understand! He wouldn't play, that's all. Who told you he'd give up that money for a dame, even if she was his wife?"

Ginn didn't speak.

He glanced round at Daphne, but didn't take much notice of her. She sat on the upright chair, close to the large packing case which served as a table. She felt stiff, her legs ached, the hard wooden seat was a kind of torture in itself. Her hair was untidy, where she'd kept poking her fingers through it. Now and again she shivered, because it was surprisingly cold down here; the cold and her nerves and her fears worked together. She hadn't had anything to eat or to drink, and her mouth was parched. Some of the time, she felt as if she was sitting on a billowy air cushion, another time as if she was sitting on rocks as hard as those on which Tony Reedon's body had been smashed.

The battle, now, was between the man and this short, heavy breasted, big eyed girl with the beautiful hair. The candlelight glistened on that hair, and on the little rhine stone clip she used to fasten it back from her forehead. Obviously the girl Gladys was frightened of Ginn, but she fought both her fear and the man with a kind of scared defiance.

Ginn hadn't spoken for so long that Gladys moved abruptly, and said: "Maybe he'll be glad to get rid of her!"

Daphne winced.

"And there's the other thing," Gladys went on spitefully. "He hadn't got a dime, see. Couldn't even pay the bus fare to the Bank—that's where I told him to book to, not near St. Paul's, see." She added that with an almost pathetic attempt to be ingratiating without humbling herself. "What makes you so sure he's got the other money and the sparklers?"

"He's got it all," Ginn said. "Must have dumped it, and can't get back to it. Don't talk to me. Before now I've known where a fortune in ice was waiting, but didn't dare to go and pick it up. He's scared in case he's tailed to the money, that's all. If I get my hands on him, I'll make him talk."

"Well, he wouldn't chance it."

"We've got to get him."

"Just tell me how," Gladys said, with a touch of venom. "Show me how clever you are."

"We'll get him," Ginn told her, "and we won't have any of your lip, or I'll smack you down." His eyes glittered, but he didn't strike her; and something told Daphne Mallow that the other girl's fears had eased. Hers hadn't, and nothing Ginn said gave her a moment's respite from the nagging dread of what might happen next. "I've got to get him alive, and got to make him talk," Ginn was saying. "The best way is to keep his wife here. If he thinks she'll get hurt, he'll talk all right."

"*He wouldn't come to see her!*" Gladys almost screeched. "Can't you get that into your thick head?"

"We'll find him," Ginn said. "We've damned well got to find him." He moved towards the door, but didn't open it at first, just stood with his hands in the pockets of his mackintosh. "You look after Mallow's wife. Nothing to eat, nothing to drink, understand? She might know where he's hiding out."

Daphne said hoarsely: "No, I don't, I swear I don't."

"I could find a way to make you remember," Ginn said, with quiet menace. "Glad, go out, make sure no one's about. I don't want to run into any coppers."

There was just room for Gladys to pass. She squeezed by, but before she could open the door, Ginn grabbed at her hair and pulled her head back. Their faces were very close together.

"And don't feed her, understand? Don't get soft hearted."

"Not after living with you," Gladys said from the back of her throat. "I wouldn't know how."

He let her go. She pulled at the heavy door, grunting with the effort, but he made no attempt to help her. When the door was open, only darkness showed; and for the first time Daphne had some idea how long she had been here. It was pitch dark; *pitch*. By day, there had been some grounds for daring to hope, but now – she would be here all the night.

She might be here for the next day, for day after day after day. She wanted to scream.

And Michael hadn't come, Michael hadn't tried to help, hadn't cared.

That was the agonising thing; not that this man was so sure that Michael had the money.

She had almost forgotten the story she had heard in the train, Ben Norris's unstoppable flow of words, the talk of other people in the carriage. Whatever had happened up to tonight seemed to have been cut out of her life. There was this moment, fear of Ginn, and now the torment of knowing that Michael had left her to her fate. She had tried to tell herself that he hadn't believed Gladys, but that hadn't really helped.

Her mouth ached with thirst, and she felt sick with hunger. She'd only pecked at her food during the weekend, just a little three times a day had kept her going; she hadn't had anything since twelve o'clock, not even that cup of tea. She was dizzy, too, and knew that if she stood up, she wouldn't be able to keep her balance.

Gladys went out.

Ginn, hands still in his pockets, moved towards Daphne.

It was the last thing she had expected, and it made her try to get to her feet. Doing so, she swayed. He pulled his hands out of his pockets, and she saw a scarf in them. *Was he going to strangle her?* Panic made her heart thump. She tried to back away, but came up against the wall.

"Keep still," he ordered. He slipped the scarf over her head, and then tied it tightly against her lips; the knot kept her lips parted, and pressed against her teeth. "While we're away," he said, "you do some thinking. You'll be okay, when we know where your husband is." He pulled her up, grabbed her wrists, and tied them together behind her. Then he stood back. "Don't waste your time trying to get out, you can't." He gripped the top of her right arm with his powerful hand, and forced her to move. "Not from where I'm going to put you," he added, and thrust her towards the corner cupboard.

He opened the door of the cupboard and pushed her inside.

She could not even scream.

He slammed the door and blackness enveloped her.

He pulled at the door, to make sure it was closed, then moved away, blew out the candle and nipped the glowing tip, an oddly fastidious gesture which prevented the smell from the smouldering wick. Now, he went to the heavy, concealed door, and pulled it open. From here, he could see the stretch of starlit blackness and the glow in the sky from the powerful lights at the sides and the tops of buildings.

The door creaked; and closed.

He heard a flurry of movement.

"The cops are coming," Gladys breathed.

Chapter Thirteen

A Killer On The Run

Lefty Ginn stood still for a split second, closed and locked the door, put the loose brick back, then moved forward across the basement without its roof. He could not see over the top without standing on tiptoe, but there were some odd pieces of concrete at one spot, and he climbed on to this and looked across the waste land. At three different points – straight ahead, to the right and to the left – he could see clusters of lights. If there were more, the high wall hid them. The lights were all similar: bright, intensely white, and with short, stubby beams. He knew, as well as Gladys, that the police were searching as they converged upon this spot.

"Up and over," he said urgently.

"That girl—" Gladys began.

"Get up!"

Ginn backed away, put his hand at Gladys's waist, and hoisted her. She muttered something he didn't catch. He gave her a push, to make sure that she was safely on the top, then hauled himself up and over. They stood together looking at the lights, the nearest of which were a hundred yards or so away.

Now, they saw more.

Several cars were gathered together at vantage points, and headlights were shining, bright near the lamps, pale a long way off; they filled most of the ruined area with light of some kind. Here and there were dark patches, the nearest between the left hand cluster of lights and the one straight ahead.

"Creep along by the wall," Ginn said. "Don't run, just go quietly. Don't make any sound. Keep going." He made her go ahead of her, and a moment later, he said: "I'm not going to let them catch you or me—alive," he added after a pause.

The word "alive" hovered on the still night air.

Sounds came from the police; and now the figures of big men showed against the diffused beams of the headlamps. The torch light seemed very bright. There was a scuffling sound, as of footsteps; noises which suggested that the police were kicking at rubble, to make sure heaps were not concealing doorways or hiding places. It would take a hundred police to cover the area properly, and there were no more than thirty here, as far as Ginn could judge.

To get through the line of approaching men, he had a hundred yards to travel. The gap between the two groups was slowly getting narrower, but the police weren't moving quickly; they were going slowly and deliberately, making sure that they missed nothing.

The wall still gave Ginn and the girl a little cover.

Gladys kicked against a stone, and stumbled; only a little noise came, but to them it sounded loud. She felt her arm grabbed, and Ginn shook her savagely.

"Keep quiet!" he hissed.

She looked round at him, and for the first time saw that he had a knife in his hand.

There were, in fact, thirty four policemen, including Roger West, coming across the ruins.

Roger knew that to comb the waste land thoroughly, at least twice as many were needed, but provided Ginn didn't discover what was happening, thirty four should be enough. The honeycomb of little basements and cellars made the going difficult. Here and there, police had to walk along narrow brick walls, careful not to slip, in order to cross a basement and make sure that no one was hiding there. Every door was closely examined, to see whether it had been opened lately or not; hinges thick with rust were put under the glare of torches, for any traces of oil.

They came across piles of rubbish, cycle tyres, a rusty kettle, old shoes, some old clothes; the carcases of birds; the skeleton of a dog which had crawled here to die.

Roger was in the middle group.

He was in the lead, and assessing the danger spots. He could see two places where anyone who meant to try to get away would make the attempt; one on his right, one on his left. Sergeant Parker had told him what the terrain was like there – very broken and battered, the damage so great that even the walls between the cellars and basements had been broken down; it was really like one huge hole in the ground, divided by partly ruined walls. That was a danger spot. Roger went towards it, carrying a torch, watching the dark shadows cast by men, bricks, walls, door frames; everything that was left after the long dead holocaust.

The scuffling sounds seemed very loud. Traffic, a long way off, made only a background hum. A man near by breathed with a Wortleberry rumble. A Yard man lit a cigarette; there wasn't any point in saying he shouldn't; they could be seen a mile off, as it was.

Roger headed for that dark spot. The red light which seemed to be in mid air, marking the dangerous wall, was some way to its left.

It was so placed that car headlights couldn't reach it, and there wasn't time to bring mobile searchlights; by the time wires and cables were rigged, the chance would be gone.

Sergeant Parker came towards him as he reached the edge of the huge hole.

"Very nasty and treacherous here, sir. If you're going down, I'd better lend you a hand."

"Right, thanks. What's the lay out?"

"Loose bricks and stuff all over the place, and some big holes—we had a chase over here five months ago, might have been six; man went down a pot hole, and broke his leg in three places."

"Bad luck," Roger said absently. "I'll get down, and lend you a hand."

He went down, dropped easily on to the floor of a cellar which had only the one wall, and then gave the uniformed sergeant a hand. By then, he was beginning to feel heavy hearted, more than ever fearful for the girl whom he should have followed. He remembered seeing her as she had entered the platform at Hoole, moving with easy freedom, smartly dressed, wholesome. "Nice", Janet had said; and just about as far removed from Ginn as any girl could be. She might know that her husband was a murderer, she might be ready and eager to help him escape the consequences, but that didn't make her bad; most people would give her full marks for it.

It was remote from the rest of the men, down here; a kind of catacomb open to the night sky.

"Gap in the wall over there, sir." Parker shone his torch, and proved to be right. "Very loose rubble about here, too, you could easily rick your ankle."

"I'll be careful."

Roger picked his way across the rubble strewn ground, climbed through the hole in the wall, and shone his torch about the next cellar. The walls of this were broken, too. He saw a shadow move.

He hissed: *"Stop!"*

The two men stood with thumping hearts, looking at the spot where the shadow had moved. Imagination? A rat, a cat, a dog? There was no sound and no other movement to attract their attention, and they went on again. It was almost impossible to move without making a noise here, because of so much loose rubble; but if that was true of them, it was true of anyone else who might be there.

It was very dark, outside the beams of their torches. Roger's struck part of a wall, and then, as he moved it slowly, fell away into a hole; the beam was lost before it reached another wall.

Parker said: "Better get another couple of chaps, sir, hadn't we?"

"Be a good idea. I—*hush!*"

He heard a sound, as of someone kicking against loose bricks; another, like a scuffle. He could hear his own heart thumping, and see Parker's torch quivering, as they stared through the distant hole.

Then he heard a different sound; a squeal, like a rabbit before it was killed; and another, softer movement in the rubble.

"Send a signal for help," he whispered to the sergeant. "Flash an SOS. Then go round the far side."

"Right, sir," breathed Parker.

He flashed his torch, then began to move – and he went too quickly. Roger heard a gasp, a fall, a rumble of falling bricks. As it quietened, he listened intently, but heard only the sound of Sergeant Parker trying to get up.

"All right, Parker?"

"Twisted—twisted my knee," Parker called back huskily. "Can't—can't move, sir."

"Keep still, then," Roger called softly.

Ginn would know he was on his own now, but he didn't think much about that. He couldn't get the sound of that squeal out of his mind; it might be a stifled scream, of a woman; of Daphne Mallow. He found himself clenching his teeth: Parker didn't want to stay, but an order was an order. The mistake had been to come here with only one man; but they'd had the whole area to cover.

He crept across the ground, towards the hole in the wall. He trod on tiny stones and on pieces of crumbling cement which gave way beneath him. He reached the hole. If he judged the sounds right, someone was very close to him; and could see the beam of his torch. He moved again, very cautiously, wedging the torch down in a hole in a heap of bricks, keeping it waist high. It covered the big hole, and part of the empty cellar beyond it. Then he crept to the far side of the hole, and stood quite still.

There it was: the sound of breathing.

Roger could see the top of the wall, solid just here, against the bright pin points of the stars. He stretched up his hands, clutched the top, and began to haul himself up. His left elbow hurt. If he made too much noise, he might bring trouble upon himself swiftly and dangerously; but he hoisted himself high, until his head was on a level with the top of the wall; and next moment, just above it.

If anyone was there, and were to glance this way, Roger's head would show against the glow in the sky.

The only sound was that breathing: his and one other's, as far as he could judge, just *one*. He made a greater effort and, elbows bent and strain his arms and shoulders almost unbearable, looked over the wall and down. The torchlight shone, bright and clear.

He saw movement!

A man darted across the hole, to get from one side to the other, and nearer freedom; just a man, on his own. His face showed for a split second, as a pale, blurred shape. He was looking towards the torch and the hole, not towards Roger. The eyes glinted as the light caught them.

The light glinted on his knife, too.

He was alone; and it was a hundred to one that it was Ginn; Roger thought of him as Ginn – the ruthless, heartless killer.

Roger hauled himself up to the top of the wall, and prepared to swing over. If the man got away, he would probably lose himself in the labyrinthine streets of London; east, west, north, or south. He had to be caught *now*. He was moving fast, taking his chance, not caring so much about the noise he made.

Roger poised for a moment on the wall.

Ginn glanced up.

He saw Roger, and checked his movement, then spun round. He stood with the knife poised, almost at shoulder height, as if he would fling it like a javelin. Both were utterly still, Roger crouching and ready to leap down, offering Ginn a large, close target for the sharp blade of his knife. There wasn't time to call out, there would be no time for others to get here.

Roger said: "Drop that knife."

Ginn didn't move.

It was going to be a fight, at best – if he could avoid the knife, or serious injury, it would be hand-to-hand, vicious and deadly.

They were poised only for a second; it seemed to be for an age. Not far off, whistles shrilled out and men shouted; Parker was probably still flashing his SOS. But that was in another world, a long way off.

Ginn flung his arm, and the knife blade glinted. Roger ducked. There was no sound of a flying knife, no clatter; it had been a feint.

It worked, for it put Roger off his balance; now, he had to go down. He leapt, desperately. Ginn was standing and crouching, bracing himself with the knife held for a sweeping blow upwards into Roger's stomach. Without seeing the blade, Roger guessed what the man would try to do.

He threw himself a little to the right, the direction in which Ginn had been going.

He felt a sharp pain in his left arm, then hit the ground, and rolled over. He was up in a trice, grabbing at Ginn, who moved with the speed of a fox. Roger missed, then grabbed again while getting to his feet. The light shone on the man who was moving fast towards the distant darkness. Roger got to his feet and bellowed: *"Get him! There he goes!"*

It didn't stop Ginn, but it made him swing round. He flung the knife. Roger saw it flicker as it left his hand; this was no feint. He ducked. The knife flew high, but dodging it lost him precious seconds; when he straightened up Ginn was out of the range of the light; but his footsteps were clear, and he went swiftly, as if he knew every inch of the waste land.

"This way!" Roger roared. *"This—"*

He kicked against a brick, and pitched forward. As he fell, he turned towards his right shoulder, to save the left elbow from getting another knock; and as he fell, he knew that he had let the man get away. He hit the ground, and rolled over. In spite of the precautions, he banged his elbow; it was hard not to cry out in pain, which slowed him down. When he got up, he staggered, and was dazed. He could hear Ginn a good way off, and could also hear other sounds, of men running, whistles shrilling. Some of the police were heading this way, but they wouldn't be in time.

Would they?

Roger dared to hope, as he stood up, shaking his head to try to free himself from pain. He turned slowly towards the torch which lodged in the wall.

He was out of the hunt, and he'd lost Ginn – as he was losing everyone today. He felt sick, partly with pain, as much with mortification. He retrieved the torch and stood with it for a moment, while men hailed him; some had headed for the light of his torch.

He remembered that little rabbit's squeal, and he thought of Daphne Mallow. If he should find her body, if he should find her dead with a knife wound—

He swung the torch round. Its beam fell on something yellow, and he remembered Mallow's description of Gladys's jumper. He moved forward, all other thought driven away. The light shone on the girl's black hair, and made it shine, on her legs, her skirt, her arms – and on her back. There, he saw a dark patch on the bright yellow of the jumper, just about the position of the heart.

A moment later, Roger was kneeling by Gladys Domwell's side; and the wet of blood was on his fingers. He had to pull down the top of her gloves to feel her pulse, a soft, fabric glove; had she made it herself, with much pride?

The man she had loved and lived with had done this.

Her pulse was still, although when Roger shone the torch into her face, something of her boldness showed; so did something of the great vitality which she had possessed, and which Ginn had cut down as a farmer would cut corn.

But where was Daphne Mallow?

Chapter Fourteen

The Search

"You ought to lay off a bit, Handsome," the police surgeon said. "That cut in your arm's nothing, but you look all in, and you sound as if you're trying to reach the moon. These chaps can search for the woman just as well as you can. You want a clear head in the morning."

Roger said: "I know, that's the common sense of it. Only I'm not in a common sense mood tonight." He lit a cigarette as he finished, and looked towards the torch beams, which were now like glow worms which moved all the time. "If he'll do that to one, he won't hesitate to do it to another. That girl was working for him."

"Nothing you can do about her," the police surgeon reasoned. "I wonder what makes 'em team up with devils like Ginn?"

Roger didn't answer.

He watched as two ambulance men, who had made their way precariously over walls, on walls, and over rubble, put Gladys on a stretcher. Her face and body was covered with a drab, off white sheet. The men lifted the stretcher, and with police to help and to guide them, started to move away. Others were already busy at the spot where she had died, going through all the routine. Photographs, measurements, footprints, finger prints – they would seek them all, with as much thoroughness as they would if they had no idea who had killed her. When Ginn was caught, the case against him would have to be proved with every item of evidence, every shred of proof.

And a lawyer, probably one paid for by the State, would try to keep him from the hangman, would fight for his life as if he deserved to live. It wasn't probable that Ginn had been here; just a certainty.

It was half an hour since he had escaped.

There was no trace of him, and little chance of finding him among the waste land and the rubble. The search would have to begin all over again; and with it, the search for Daphne Mallow.

Reinforcements were on the way from the Yard and from the Divisions, but although they would work through the night, if needs be, it would be wise to expect nothing; until the morning, at least, they weren't likely to find clues.

Pessimism? Presentiment?

"Well, I'm off," the police surgeon said. "Got a whisky flask with you?"

"Left it in my desk," Roger told him.

"Take mine," the doctor said. "And if you lose or break that flask, I'll set my wife on you!"

He thrust a flask into Roger's hand, then turned to follow the ambulance men.

Gratefully, Roger took a swig of whisky, worked it round his mouth, and then swallowed. He put the flask into his hip pocket, and wiped his mouth with the back of his hand. On the instant, he pictured Janet and Richard, and in spite of himself he grinned; even chuckled. Richard's sheepish air, and the way he had ducked out of the room would help to wipe out a lot of ugly pictures on his mind.

Roger squared his shoulders, and climbed out of the pit, without looking at the painstaking men who were busy with their seemingly pointless work. Now, the whole stretch of land was pinpointed with lights, which moved constantly; a dozen cars were shining their headlamps across the rubble. The pessimistic feeling of uselessness had gone; thought of Richard and Janet had cheered him up. He was a copper, wasn't he? A copper's job took him into the ugliness and the brutality of life; if the man in the street knew everything, he'd take a pretty jaundiced view of the world. No one ever would know everything. No one would even know what it was like to be a C.I.D.

man who was ready to blame himself for one girl's death and another's disappearance.

Yet the police surgeon had something.

There was nothing that others couldn't do: it was a case of searching, here and throughout London, for some sign of Daphne Mallow or of Ginn. Tomorrow might demand a lot of reserves of strength and logic which he wouldn't have if he tired himself out. He was lucky he hadn't damaged himself badly. Sergeant Parker had gone off in a police car, with a badly wrenched knee – an old trouble which the fall had re-awakened. He, Roger, might have been out of action; or dead.

He heard a hail.

"That Mr. West, sir?"

"Yes."

"Message for you, sir."

"Thanks. Coming!"

He quickened his step, able to walk without the light of the torch now that he was nearer the group of cars. The headlamps turned the darkness of desolation into a spurious brightness. The one with the longest range caught Roger full in the face, when he made a slight detour to avoid a wall. It cast a fantastically long shadow across the ruins, and the tip of the shadow of his head fell a few feet away from the doorway which looked like solid brick, faintly red from the danger sign.

The policeman nearest to Daphne Mallow, at that moment, was Roger West.

He drew farther away.

"This car, sir," a man called out. He was one of two on duty by the cars, uniformed, deep voiced. He touched the peak of his hat. "Mr. Cortland, sir."

"Thanks."

Roger slid into the seat next to the driver and picked up the radio telephone. The time when a message by walkie talkie was both novel and urgent had gone; this might be about anything.

"West speaking."

"'Bout time," Cortland said, but he wasn't serious about that. "Any luck with Mallow's wife?"

Sharply, Roger said: "No."

"Pity," Cortland said. "We've got Mallow looking like death warmed up, and we've had a nasty message from Ginn."

Roger began: "You've had—" and broke off.

"That's right. He phoned the GK Station. Very simple." Cortland didn't mean to be tantalising, he was just being himself. "He said that if we don't let Mallow go, he'll kill his wife. Know who Gladys Domwell is?" Cortland asked, with a kind of resentful insistence.

"Yes," said Roger gruffly. "Yes, I know. Thanks. Hold on a minute, will you?" He put the receiver down and stared across the darkness towards the East End, and the garish light towards Holborn. From here he could see the police moving about with slow and deliberate movements, a dozen torches flashing at the same time. He found himself lighting a cigarette. Then he raised the receiver again. "Hallo, Corty. Sorry. Either Ginn is more desperate than we ever thought, or he can really kill Daphne Mallow. If he can, she isn't where I thought she was."

Cortland grunted.

"What's this about Mallow looking like death?" Roger asked.

"Well, we gave him a meal—he ate as if he hadn't touched food for days!" There was real astonishment in Cortland's voice. "Just shovelled it in. He said he spent all the cash he had on a few things he had to buy. We thought the food would quieten him down, but not a bit of it. He's been on the rampage. Why don't we find his wife, what do we think he gave himself up for? He didn't kill anyone, he can prove it, he wants a solicitor. And he wants to go and look for his wife," Cortland went on; and sniffed. "Tell you one thing, Handsome—I dunno whether he's right about his innocence, but I'd say he loves his wife the way I ought to love mine."

Roger didn't even think about making a quip.

"I'll come and have another word with him," he said, "he might give me an angle."

"What about the search, then? We've had two urgent calls for help tonight, and can't send more men out to Divisions because of the concentration round St. Paul's."

"Sorry." Roger was suddenly brisk. "I'd like more on that job, not less. Be nice to everybody. Or tell them the simple truth," he added savagely. "That the woman—"

"Listen, Handsome," Cortland broke in, "why don't you take it easy? They'll finish the job as well without you as with you. And why don't you stop blaming yourself? Ginn pushed you in front of a train, otherwise you wouldn't have lost Mallow's wife. Stop being Atlas."

There was a pause. Then: "Thanks, Corty," Roger said, and rang off.

When he drew his hand across his forehead it was wet with sweat. He didn't move, but took out the whisky flask and took another tot. When he wiped his mouth with the back of his hand, he didn't think of Richard. He got out of the car, conscious of the curious gaze of the policeman. He nodded, but didn't speak. Then he walked across to confer with a Divisional man and two sergeants.

Nothing had been found.

"We know the direction Ginn came from," Roger said. "Let's make sure we cover that."

No one else suggested that he should go home, but he knew what was on their minds. Yet nothing could have drawn him away from the ruins, except news of Ginn. There was no news – of Ginn, or of the girl. Every place Ginn was known to frequent, every friend or contact he had in the East End, was interviewed that night; it was as if a vow of silence had been imposed upon them all.

Gladys Domwell's sister swore she knew nothing more.

By half past one, they had nearly finished the search near St. Paul's. Policemen were human beings, with human limitations, and they began to flag in spirit and in body. Many of them had been working most of the day, and had volunteered for this extra duty. Others had lost the stimulus of excitement when they knew that Ginn had escaped. No one could be sure that the other woman was here. Yet they were all conscious of the way West drove them on, and something in his tension kept them moving.

It was a quarter to two when a whistle shrilled out; a signal of discovery.

"Not much doubt about it, this is where they were," a man said to Roger. He was in the outer cellar, and a dozen torches were lodged on the walls, shining down on the half dozen police making the search. "That's the murdered woman's compact, all right—G.D., too much of a coincidence to think there was anyone else here with those initials, isn't it?"

Roger said: "I should think so." He turned the cheap brass compact over in his hand. The initials were large, it was one of the "souvenir from Southend" pieces, available with almost every combination of two initials. The faint smell of perfumed powder came from it. In the pale red glow from the "danger" wall and the light of a torch, he could see only one set of fingerprints; someone with a small hand. He held the compact by the edges, and then put it carefully in a white envelope. "How'd she come to drop it, I wonder? Did she have a handbag?" He answered the question himself. "No." Then his voice rose. "That's a thing to look for— Gladys Domwell's handbag. Find out what it was like, whether she had it with her tonight, if not, what happened to it? Flash that to the Yard, will you? See if Mallow knows."

"Right away."

"Thanks."

"The footprints aren't very clear," said another man. "Man and a woman, but they trampled all over the place. Could be two women, I suppose, we'd tell better in day light."

"Go round the walls, tap them all thoroughly," Roger said. "Don't miss even half a chance."

"We won't."

Men began to go round the walls, using wooden hammers, tapping every square foot for a hollow sound. They found none, although they actually tapped the movable brick.

Now and again, the tapping set up a tremor in the wall which loomed high above them. No one noticed it.

Inside, almost sealed up in that cupboard, Daphne did not even know the police were there. She was bitterly cold. Fear and terror had merged into a kind of stupor. Every now and again she had a flare of horror, when she thought she heard a sound, and prayed that the door would open.

It didn't. Her legs, her feet, her whole body ached.

She began to wonder whether Ginn was coming back.

When a man looked as if he had the burden of the world on his shoulders even *in* sleep, it was bad. Janet West knew that Roger felt as badly as he could. She stood by the bedside, looking down. He hadn't stirred when she'd got up, just after seven, to start getting breakfast. She knew he'd come home in the early hours, but wasn't sure what time; he'd hardly disturbed her. Now, he slept with his lips tightly closed, and with a sharp groove between his eyebrows, which were drawn together slightly. She knew him as well as a wife could know her husband; and she knew that when he looked like this, it was because things were going gravely wrong.

The fair stubble on his cheeks and chin was smeared with dust and dirt; he hadn't washed before falling into bed, a measure of physical fatigue. One hand, over the bedspread, had two nasty scratches; the nails were dirty – unusual with him – and one was broken. She knew that there was nothing she could do, except be herself. She wasn't worried, beyond the ordinary worry of a wife for the man she loves because things are going badly; but he'd get through this bad spell as he had others. Of all his qualities, the one which served him best was refusal to give up. Refusal? It was virtually an impossibility.

"*Mum*," one of the boys whispered, so softly that she couldn't be sure which one it was. "*Mum, can we come in?*"

It was a little after eight. The Yard hadn't telephoned yet, and there was no need to wake Roger until there was a call. Janet went out, so preoccupied that she didn't at first understand the suppressed excitement of the boys; or guess why the newspapers were in their hands, one in each.

"*Look!*" Richard almost squealed.

"What—" began Janet, and then saw Martin's news paper, held out towards her so that she could see Roger's photograph. "What is it?" she exclaimed.

"He was pushed in front of a *train*," breathed Martin.

"If I could find that man, I'd kill him!" Richard lost the battle to keep his voice low.

"Quiet," breathed Janet. "Let's get away from here."

She led the way to the head of the stairs, the boys following her as day old clucks would follow a hen. She groped for the top step, and started down, still looking at the newspaper. In the hall, she read the main parts of the story. It was nearly all there; the two men battered to death in Hoole, the murder of an unnamed girl near St. Paul's, Ginn's escape, the description of the encounter between Ginn and Roger – in heavy black type and largely guesswork – and the fact that Daphne Mallow was missing.

"Do you think Dad will be awake before we go to school?" Richard asked.

Janet made herself put the paper down.

"I don't know. You mustn't worry him, anyhow, he has enough on his mind as it is. Now finish dressing, if I don't hurry you'll be late for school."

They'd left the house when the telephone rang, other urgent matters on their minds.

Would Roger go to the Yard as quickly as possible, several urgent matters were awaiting his attention, and the Assistant Commissioner wanted to see him in his office at half past nine.

It was now twenty minutes to.

Roger had a quick, cold bath, a bad shave, and nothing like enough breakfast, he was in too much of a hurry. He did everything with a speed and tension which told the same story as his expression when he had been asleep. Janet didn't obtrude, didn't ask questions. He kissed her with that little extra vigour which told of grateful understanding, and at nine fifteen was getting into the car which had been sent for him from the Yard. Not having his own car was a nuisance, but it didn't make a lot of difference. As he lit his first cigarette of the morning, he looked back; Janet and the house were out of sight; only the neat brick houses and neat, hedged-in gardens of the neighbours were there. He wished he hadn't been so short with Janet.

"Nice morning, sir," the driver said.

"Yes. Fine."

In fact, it was already warm, and the temperature would probably be up in the eighties today; hot, for London. It wasn't sticky yet, not in the way it could be. Roger eased his collar, and wished he'd put on a lighter suit. Then the car swung into the Yard, and the first thing he saw was his own green Wolseley.

"Did you know my car was here?" he asked.

"It wasn't when I left, sir."

"Hm," said Roger.

Wortleberry must have had a driver bring it up; unless Bradding, who had stayed in Hoole, had come with a report. Roger put that out of his mind. It was exactly half past nine, and Sir Guy Chatworth didn't like being kept waiting.

He'd have to wait for five minutes.

Only Eddie Day, one of nature's ugly men, was in the office. His big, protruding teeth seemed to force his lips apart, as he greeted: "Didn't you know the Old Man was waiting for you?"

"Just ring him, and tell him I'll be half an hour or so," Roger said tartly; and felt the morning's first moment of relaxation when Eddie took him seriously; and was horrified.

"Listen, Handsome, you can't do a thing like that. You must be—" He stopped, saw Roger's grin, and became aggrieved.

He turned stiffly back to his own desk, and Roger glanced through the reports on his.

There was nothing in that mattered.

Gladys Domwell had had a green handbag with her; her married sister, with whom she lived in a tiny house off the Whitechapel Road, was quite sure of that, and Mallow had confirmed it. She'd had a few pounds, because she worked with the manufacturing glove maker, who paid his staff on Thursday. There were other notes about what she had in her bag, but the important thing was to find the bag itself.

There was nothing about Daphne Mallow.

Mallow's mood hadn't changed.

There was nothing new about Ginn.

At twenty minutes to ten Roger tapped at the door of Chatworth's office. He uttered a silent prayer: that Chatworth wouldn't be in a hectoring or a critical mood. He could be the world's best boss, and he could borrow characteristics of the Devil. He probably had no idea of what Roger was feeling, if he had he'd almost certainly soft pedal. With the morning newspapers and a virtually blank report sheet on his desk, he would much more likely bark.

"Come in!"

Roger squared his shoulders, and opened the door.

Chatworth sat at his flat topped desk in the room furnished with black glass and chromium, looking like a farmer on holiday. He was positively angelic, actually smiled, waved a hand, and said: "Come in, come in, West, glad you made it. You know Superintendent Wortleberry, don't you?"

Wortleberry sat squeezed in a chair which was inches too small for him. He was ill at ease, obviously glad to see a familiar face, and had an open suitcase by his feet. On a sheet of crumpled newspaper on Chatworth's desk lay a big rock. It was the size of a very large pear, ugly, jagged, and stained with a brownish colour.

Chapter Fifteen

Wortleberry's Finds

"Don't get up, Superintendent, don't get up," Chatworth urged benignly. "Come and sit down, West."

Wortleberry looked relieved, with reason, for getting out of the tubular steel arms of his chair was a major operation. He looked pasty besides Chatworth's brick brown face, a colourless man against the A.C.'s colourfulness; but there was something dogged and likeable about him.

"Thought I'd come up myself, there were one or two things we found down at Hoole," he said. "Drove your car. Thought you could do with it. Hope you don't mind."

Roger made a point of shaking hands.

"I'm really grateful—lost without it. Thanks. What's this?"

He eyed the stone. He knew what it was, within the limits of probability, but it would be unkind to rob Wortleberry of the opportunity of explaining. He sat down. Already he felt much better; the day was really a new day.

For the time being the fate of Daphne Mallow was at the back of his mind.

"Glad I did the right thing," snuffled Wortleberry. "Well, that's blood, you can tell that. Had a group test—Group A. The dead man in the cottage, what's his name, Silver, was Group A. So was Reedon's." He breathed heavily, and prepared to deliver himself again. "Some prints on the stone, too."

West said softly: "Fine. Mallow's?"

"No."

"Whose?"

"Ginn's."

It really was a new day. There was a lot to do, the pressure of the search for the missing girl hadn't relaxed, but if there'd been any doubt before, there wasn't now; they had Lefty Ginn. Ginn had fingered the rock which had killed his own accomplice in crime, or else had killed Reedon.

It was like a flash of light in a dark room.

The flash faded.

Roger didn't speak at first, and knew that the others were waiting for him to comment. They watched, intently. He had a new thought – not wholly new, but sharply at variance with the satisfaction that had come with the discovery of those finger prints. The flash of relief hadn't lasted long.

"What's on your mind?" Chatworth asked. "Didn't you expect to find that Ginn had been there? Eh? Disappointed that they weren't Mallow's prints?"

"No, sir," Roger said slowly, formally. "Hardly that. But Ginn's— he's giving himself away in every way he can. I don't get it."

Wortleberry snuffled.

"Don't *get you*," Chatworth said briefly.

There was no need for further time to think; Roger understood his own doubts, his own reaction, his own bewilderment; several of the things that had puzzled him before came into sharp relief.

"We were on to Ginn from the moment we knew that Chips Silver had been killed," he said. "We didn't worry whether Ginn or someone else had killed Chips, we just went for Ginn because it was obviously on the cards. We've picked up a hundred men that way. But after that, there was the girl, Gladys Domwell. All reports about her are the same: she's no fool. Yet what happened? Ginn didn't hide the fact that he was back in the East End, and that she was his girl. Ginn's been out of circulation for years, and suddenly comes back. Why? And why did Gladys talk as freely as she did to Mallow? You know about that, sir, Superintendent Wortleberry doesn't. She told

Mallow that Lefty Ginn had his wife, remember. That was taking a hell of a chance, wasn't it—telling Mallow his name. The girl couldn't be sure that Mallow would go where she wanted him, and it didn't work out that way. He came to us, and named Lefty."

Chatworth competed with Wortleberry; and won.

"Hm, yes, I see what you mean," he rumbled. "Don't see where it will get us, though. The girl slipped up. She may have believed that Mallow would be frightened of the name

of Ginn. She—" Chatworth straightened up. "Yes, of course, that's it. She used the name to frighten Mallow, thought that it was familiar to him."

"Might a' been," Wortleberry observed daringly.

Roger found himself lighting a cigarette.

"Yes. Yes," he repeated more briskly. "Well, we haven't heard everything Mallow can tell us, we've known that for some time. And whatever the reason—"

"Puzzling thing, that Ginn killed his light o' love," said Chatworth, who sometimes revealed a Puritanical reluctance to call a spade a spade. "If Ginn knew she'd named him, and he thought Mallow had come to the police and also named him, he'd feel pretty vicious."

Roger said: "Yes, he would," very slowly. He kept them waiting for a few seconds, then pulled himself together. "Sorry, sir. Well, with any luck we'll have Ginn today."

"Hope we do," said Wortleberry, and looked almost coy. He glanced at Chatworth, as if seeking permission to go on. With men from the provincial forces Chatworth could be cherubic, and obviously he liked Wortleberry. "There's something else," purred Wortleberry. "Your man Bradding found that, as a matter of fact. There's a set of prints in the cottage which don't square up with anyone known to have been there."

Roger said: "A man's?"

"Yes. Biggish chap, I'd say. Not Reedon's, Mallow's, Ginn's, or what's-his-name—Silver, isn't it, Chips Silver. Ah. Carpenter or something. Not the gardener's, either. Look," added Wortleberry, and bent low, grunting and snuffling, to pick something else out of the suitcase. "See?"

These were dampish photographs of fingerprints, clear evidence of the high pressure at which the Hoole police had worked.

"As far as we can tell they were made about the same time—in the dust of the bedroom, anyhow, and that dust must've come from the ceiling when the hole was made. So it's pretty certain that unknown chap was there when the others were—or just after. Always the same," Wortleberry added, permitting himself a little grumble. "Either you get too many prints or too few. Too many, this time, we could do without that chap; but he's been there." He didn't actually smile, but his tone softened as he went on: "Not yours, either, Mr. West, Bradding's sure of that!"

"A complete newcomer on the scene," Roger said, "and a man with big fingers."

"That's it. Might be a big man altogether, but you're right—the only thing we know for certain is the big fingers. Bradding and some of my chaps are having another go at the cottage, Mr. West, I don't think they'll miss anything."

"I'll bet they won't!" Roger found himself smiling almost freely. "Anything more up your sleeve?"

"Well, not really," Wortleberry said. "I brought duplicate reports of everything. I've been trying to find a line on Reedon before he moved to Hoole. Only things at the cottage were one or two school certificates—and *this.*"

Wortleberry took out a foolscap envelope, extracted a piece of stiff paper, and presented it to Roger. It was a certificate from an Institute of Engineering, showing that a man named Rawson had served his apprenticeship as a locksmith.

"Hallo!" Roger exclaimed, as he read. "Locksmith—safe breaker. Now we've got a line. Rawson—" He glanced at Chatworth. "Mind if I get 'em moving on this?"

"I'll see to it," Chatworth said, and pressed a bell; almost on the instant his secretary came in, a middle aged woman wearing a white blouse and black skirt. He handed her the certificate. "Have that man Rawson checked, quickly—give it to Turnbull, if he's in."

"Yes, sir." The woman went out.

Roger said: "Don't tell me there's anything else."

"Just a bit," said Wortleberry almost smugly. "If Reedon had a cache at the cottage, and was a crook, it looks as if Mallow found out. Had a bit of luck—found a letter on the beach which must have been washed out of Reedon's pocket. Smudged, but legible."

He produced the note, and Roger read: "Tony, I'm in a bad fix. Will you see me tonight, midnight, at your place? Don't want Daff to know. And could you find fifty quid, just to tide me over? Michael."

Got a smell of blackmail, somehow," Wortleberry surmised.

"Could have," Roger agreed.

Wortleberry broke off, almost in alarm; it was quite clear that he had been talking much as he would to his own men, and suddenly pulled himself up.

"See what I mean," he added in some confusion.

"We do indeed," said Chatworth briskly. He smoothed down the fringe of grizzled hair at the back of his head, and ran a palm over his large bald patch. "Well, we need to know who the chap with big fingers was. That won't take long if he's known to us. What do you recommend next, West?"

"The thing that worries me most is Daphne Mallow," Roger said. "We've got to face this threat, that Ginn will kill her if we don't let Mallow go."

Chatworth didn't speak.

"Chap can't think we'll knuckle under to a threat like that," Wortleberry protested.

"We want Ginn, and we want him as quickly as we can get him." The sharpness of Roger's voice stopped the words from sounding too formal. "Ginn thinks that Mallow has the money, and that he can make Mallow turn it over. Judging from the reports on Mallow's attitude about his wife, he's probably right, if he—"

"If he has it," Wortleberry put in. "Lot of things suggest he's on his uppers, don't they? Wouldn't be, if he'd lifted that cash."

"What about that envelope with the fifty one pounds in?" West asked.

Wortleberry opened his mouth, and closed it again, almost fish like. He flushed, and then stooped down again, grinning, to take something else from the suitcase.

"Forgot that," he said. "It had a few smudges and two lots of prints, Charley Ray's, the postman's, and the same big prints as we found in the dust at the cottage. *Not* Mallow's," Wortleberry added, with deliberate emphasis. "The new lot."

"There's considerable evidence that someone else has the money," Chatworth put in. "In statements made to you last night, West, Mallow denies having had that money, but denies nothing else. Think you can make him talk now?"

"I can have a good try," Roger said grimly. "But the basic problem's the same, whether he talks or not. Can we get Ginn? If Mallow is freed, Ginn will try to get at him. We could release Mallow, and watch. It's the old trick, but no worse because of that. We can hold Mallow if we want to, but we've a pretty logical reason to let him go. The risk is that Ginn might kill him. Provided Mallow's worried about that—"

"You really want to release Mallow, and follow him?" Chatworth was sharper.

"I'd take a lot of risks in order to get Ginn quickly," Roger said. "Ginn's the only man who knows for certain where Daphne Mallow is."

"Go and see Mallow," decided Chatworth. "See what you make of him this morning. If you'd like to be present at the interview, Superintendent, I'm sure Chief Inspector West will be glad of your advice." He was cherubic again, all sharpness dulled. "I'll see you later—no, don't worry about the exhibits, I'll have them sent down to the Chief Inspector's office."

Roger went with Wortleberry to the door. The Hoole man made an elephantine turn, to smile timid thanks at the great Assistant Commissioner, before they walked towards the stairs.

A lot had come in at once; it wasn't what Roger hoped for, but it took them a little farther. A little? Those fingerprints might come to mean everything. The unknown "Rawson" as a locksmith might, too. Rawson *alias* Reedon?

The vital thing was to make Mallow talk.

Wortleberry said: "Bit of a tiger, isn't he? Er—don't think I don't want to be helpful, but I'd much rather you handled the interview. Too many cooks, you know."

Mallow obviously hadn't slept much. He'd had a shave, and looked more together, but his eyes burned. He kept getting up from his chair, as if he couldn't stay in the same place for long. He looked more like his photograph now, with his hair standing up on end, thick and wiry, most of the effect of the brilliantine gone. His hands were continually working, he kept banging a clenched fist into the palm of his other hand.

"I tell you the only thing that matters is to find my wife. What are you doing about it? Why are you wasting time here, when every policeman on the Force ought to be on the look out!"

"A great many are," Roger said, his one concession to mildness. "Stop pacing about, and let's have the truth. You could have saved your wife by handing that money over."

"I don't know anything about the bloody money!"

"You were at the cottage when—"

"I went to see Reedon. Okay, I went to borrow some money! I'm broke, but I didn't kill anyone. When I got there, I found a chap lying at the foot of the stairs with his head bashed in. I—I looked for Tony, and couldn't see him." Mallow flung the words out, as if it were the tenth, not the first time that he had said them. "Then someone I didn't see clumped me on the back of the head. If you don't believe me, I've still got the bruise, *look!*" He lunged forward, bending almost double, to let them see the back of his head. The hair, glistening with the brilliantine, was unexpectedly thin in the centre, and there was a slight bruise; the skin was broken and there was a pink scab. "I thought I'd had it," Mallow went on, his voice now almost a screech. "I thought he was going to smash my head in, like he had the other chap's. Was I scared! When I came round, I couldn't believe I was still alive, I just couldn't believe it!" He caught his breath.

"Where were you when you came round?" Roger asked.

"In the cottage. Near the other man, with his head—That was—awful." Mallow seemed to shiver uncontrollably. "Awful. There was—there was a whacking great rat, creeping—" He closed his eyes. Wortleberry snuffled, as if in sympathy. Roger's expression didn't change; he watched every expression on Mallow's face, and in the blue eyes. "That's all," Mallow went on, much more slowly. "I went home and—and decided to run away."

"Why?"

"Haven't you got any sense? Can't you understand why—?"

"No," Roger said flatly. "If that's really what happened, in your place I would have sent for the police. Why didn't you?"

"I—I was scared."

"What makes you scared of the police?"

Mallow closed his mouth, tightly, and didn't make any attempt to answer.

"Look here, Mallow," Roger said roughly, "this man Ginn is a killer. He has your wife somewhere, so she's in acute danger. Get that into your head. We've got to know everything you can tell us. Never mind risking your own neck; if you care anything for your wife, let's have the whole truth."

Mallow said thinly: "I've told you it all."

"You haven't told us why you ran away. Why you wanted to leave your home. Let's have the truth. You killed your friend Reedon, didn't you? You banged him over the head and then pushed him over the cliff into Demon's Cove. You went to burgle his house and found the others there. Come on, let's have it!"

"It's not true," Mallow gasped. "I didn't kill Tony. He was my closest friend, why the hell should I kill him?" He paused; and it seemed for a long time. Then he burst out: *"When are you going to find my wife?* Daff, oh, Daff—"

He broke off, and there were tears in his eyes.

"Oh, he's keeping something back," Roger said to the A.C. "I wouldn't like to guess what. I would like to say he can't switch on tears as he wants to. This love for his wife could be a big act. One queer thing, if he has told us the truth."

"What's that?"

"He was knocked out in the cottage, fingered the door to get in, probably touched other things—but left no prints. Did he wear gloves, I wonder? Did he make sure he left no prints?"

"Good point," Chatworth said. "Still recommend letting him go?"

"I think it's worth a chance. If he knows where Ginn is, he'll probably lead us to him. To tail him I'll select a man who won't make any mistake, and we'll leave it until we can send look out calls to all the stations and divisions. I can't believe he'll escape—"

Roger said that as if he wasn't really at all sure.

Wortleberry said: "If you don't mind me putting a word in, Assistant Commissioner, I'd like to say that I agree with West. Er—Mr. West. Fully. I should say that Mallow and Ginn have worked together in the past, eh—er—Mr. West?"

"Could be," Roger agreed.

"Do what you think's best," conceded Chatworth, "but don't lose Mallow."

He didn't add, "Like you lost the others," but the rider seemed implicit. Wortleberry made no further comment.

Roger went down to his office, to give orders for a shadow to get ready to follow Mallow, and to arrange a general lookout for him. He arranged for two men to do the tailing, but knew, as did Chatworth and everyone else, Mallow could give them the slip if he really wanted to; any man could.

One question stood out. If Ginn didn't feel sure that Mallow would get in touch with him, why had he sent that "ultimatum"?

Another: if Mallow hadn't the money, why was Ginn so sure that he had?

The importance of the unidentified fingerprint was mounting, but there was nothing in the Yard records to help; the prints were of a man without a police record.

There was no record of anyone named Rawson, either, but the Institute had records of an Anthony Rawson who'd served an apprenticeship with the Landon Lock Company; a Yard man was now checking with Landon's. Rawson had been there ten years or so ago, and was bound to be remembered by some of the staff.

Would they recognise Reedon as Rawson?

Just now, that question hardly seemed important.

Too much seemed to depend on whether Mallow and Ginn met. There was more than a solution of the case; there was the life of Daphne Mallow. That harried Roger more than anything else. Whenever he looked at her photograph he thought of Janet's words, and what he knew of the girl.

He had only known her when she was frightened.

In Ginn's hands she would be terrified.

If she was alive.

Chapter Sixteen

The Steel Cupboard

At the moment when West released Michael Mallow, Daphne Mallow was conscious.

For several hours, in the cupboard that might well become her tomb, she had been in a coma, sleep and unconsciousness merging together; at least, she had been less conscious of fear than she had when she had been fully conscious. Occasionally, she stirred and had a few moments of absolute clarity of vision; of awful understanding.

It was like being in a dark, cold hell.

She began to shiver and shake. The knot of the scarf pressed against her teeth, so that she couldn't open her mouth properly, could only try to gnaw at the cloth. She didn't try very often, for her muscles as well as her will went limp.

The air was so foul.

She sat on the cold floor part of the time, head against the wall. Each time she woke herself up she was in that position. Then she would get to her feet and kick at the steel door, until it hurt so much, and she had to stop.

She made no sound that travelled far, had no reason to hope. She would sink back into the stupor, and wake up to go through it all again, as if in a recurring nightmare.

There were other things.

Hunger; physical weakness; thirst. Her mouth was so dry that it felt hard and brittle against her tongue. There was something oily on the scarf, which made it worse. She kept trying to work her lips up and down a little, and sometimes it seemed easier; once or twice, without realising what she had done, she gnawed through a few strands of the material, and slackened the pressure slightly.

Most of the time, there was just the coldness, the silence, and the creeping fear that she was going to stay here until she died.

Outside, the police were searching the derelict land again, in the better light of day.

Roger stood outside the shop in Whitechapel, and looked up at the green painted window, with the words, *Sol Riddle, Glove maker, Special Orders, Surgical Work Done,* painted in black. He could just see the heads of some of the girls working in the shop. The door itself was open, and that was marked *Trade Only*. He went in. The whirr of sewing machines came insistently from a back room; different noises, carrying their tale of busyness, came from beyond a wooden partition which separated the Trade Counter from the workroom. A door in this partition opened before he had pressed the bell marked: *Ring.*

A flamboyant looking young man with dark, wavy hair, very heavily oiled, a teenager's dream of a pink and white complexion, and beautiful honey coloured eyes, came into the little cubicle. He seemed to fill it; it was like seeing an orchid growing on the waste land where Gladys Domwell had died. His full, beautifully shaped lips were ready to break into a smile. Large, well kept hands were ready to gesticulate. He hesitated when he saw Roger, obviously puzzled and doubting whether this was a customer.

"Good morning." His voice was pleasant, with just an overdose of nasal twang.

"Good morning," Roger said, and produced a card. "May I speak to Mr. Soloman Riddle?"

"Certainly, sir," said the flamboyant looking young man. "I am Sol Riddle. How can I help you?"

"Is there somewhere we can talk quietly, Mr. Riddle?"

Riddle glanced down at the card, and widened his eyes. He looked more puzzled, and on his guard; perhaps wary. That didn't mean a thing; in this district there was a sound chance that anyone questioned by the police would have some sense of guilt on his conscience.

"Certainly, let's go upstairs," Riddle said promptly enough. "My flat is above the workshop, Chief Inspector—*West*, isn't it?" He flashed white teeth. "Thought I'd seen your face before, Mr. West, pictures of it anyhow!" He called out: "Rachel, I shall be out for a little while, please look after things," and pushed up the flap in the counter and ushered Roger out, then into a doorway adjoining the shop, and up the stairs. "It's a small flat," he said apologetically, "just room for my poor old mother and me, don't take any notice of her if she sees us, Chief Inspector, she's stone deaf. Such a pity."

The flat and the rooms were small, but well furnished. In the room where Sol Riddle took Roger there was a large television set, a Bergere suite with royal blue cushions in its couch, and two chairs, a walnut cocktail cabinet, and a sprinkling of valuable oddments, placed with excellent taste. The carpet looked newish Persian.

"Sit down, please, and tell me what I can do for you?" invited Riddle. "Not serious trouble, I hope, is it?"

He sat down, looking less flustered.

"Very serious," Roger said flatly. "You have a girl named Gladys Domwell working for you?"

The honey coloured eyes seemed to grow larger. There was a long pause, as if Riddle was trying to grasp the significance of that, before he said: "Yes, yes, that is so. Is Gladys in trouble? Such a pity, she is a very good girl, a very good worker, one of the best in the trade. It isn't so easy to get a good girl now, not a conscientious girl. Gladys would always put her best into a job. And such a clever worker, too. If I can help her, Chief Inspector, I will be glad to."

"I'd like to talk to any of her friends, anyone she knew particularly well here."

Riddle's eyes were steady, and his hands lay motionless in his lap.

"Chief Inspector, is there trouble with that man she has been going with? That Ginn?"

Roger said sharply: "What do you know about Ginn?"

"Not very much," answered Riddle. "But when Gladys was first going with him, I warned her. I saw the man once, and I can tell a bad man, Mr. West, I knew he was one I wouldn't trust." He raised his hands expressively. "But you know how it is? Why does a girl like Gladys give herself to such a man? I wish I could tell you. My own sister, Chief Inspector, she married a no good heel, and what has he done for her? Just given her a life of misery, that's all, worry and misery and unhappiness, and he isn't even kind to her. Poor Rosie! That is what I always warn Gladys—this man will lead you that kind of life. But you couldn't do anything about it, Mr. West, she was so stubborn. People in love are stubborn, aren't they? What trouble has he got her into, Chief Inspector?"

"Did you know his reputation?"

Riddle shrugged gracefully, persuasively.

"Well, yes, you know how it is, Chief Inspector, if a man knows his way about, he gets to know things. This Ginn—why, I knew of him before he went away, good riddance, my old father said, it was a pity he wasn't hanged. I am honest with you—I knew Ginn just a little when we were both younger. In the old days he was bad, since he returned—" Sol Riddle paused, then spread his hands and shook his head. "Have you seen him, Chief Inspector? He *looks* bad, now, he even looks as if he is going bad inside, a sick man. Jaundice, I should say, my old father died from it, the years he suffered. But never mind my old father, Chief Inspector. I confess to you, Ginn came and asked me for work. I wouldn't employ such a man, but it was here he met Gladys. How is it that she fell for him? I don't know, I really don't." He paused again, then added in a flat voice: "Please, tell me what trouble it is?"

"He killed her," Roger said.

Riddle's hands, half way to his chest, stopped moving. His body went rigid. A little of the peach like colour faded from his cheeks. Then he let out a long, sad sigh, and very slowly shook his head.

"Poor old Glad," he said. "It doesn't help much to know that I warned her. But for me, perhaps they would not have met. I am sorry, Chief Inspector, very sorry; and if I can help, I will."

No one at the glove maker's was any help at all.

At a quarter to twelve Roger pulled his car up outside 27 Butt Lane, and looked up at a very different kind of building from the shop in Whitechapel. This was tall, grey, and grimed, with small windows; it had nothing at all to commend it except its position. It was actually half way along Butt Lane, although the last but two of the buildings left in it. The other had been flattened during that Great Fire of 1941. Behind it and beyond it were the flattened ruins or the skeleton walls of what had once been that mass of buildings.

Roger went in. The hall was dark and gloomy, a stone staircase offered an uninviting way up, a lift well, without the lift, was like a prison cell by the side of the stairs. On a wall, dimly illuminated from the doorway, was a panel of names and companies who had offices here. He read:

Mildmay's, Stationery and Office Furniture, H. J. Netherby, Manager.
4th Floor.

Roger pressed the lift bell; nothing happened. He pressed again, with the same result. Impatiently, he moved towards the stone steps. Each flight was long and the steps were steep, and when he passed the lift descending, at the third floor, he wished he had been more patient.

At each landing a window overlooked the flattened stretch; and from each window he could see St. Paul's, the police, the cars, the ruins. He didn't spend much time there, but quickened his pace at the last flight, to prove to himself that he was in perfect condition. At the end of it he wasn't so sure. He didn't wait to get his breath back, but tapped sharply on the frosted glass door marked:

Mildmay's
Stationery—Office Equipment
Head Office and Works: Bridgnorth

Typewriters clicked; that was the only sound. He opened the door, and saw three girls, two of them at typewriters, one at an open ledger; the girl at the ledger looked up, the others gave him a swift, curious glance and went on with their job. There was a way to sense the efficiency at a glimpse; and he saw it here. The office was small and immaculate, as bright as it could be.

It overlooked the rabbit warren of the new catacombs.

The girl at the ledger stood up, and gave him a formal smile.

"Good morning. Can I help you?"

"Is Mr. Netherby in?"

"Have you an appointment, sir?"

"No." He slid out his card. "Ask him to see me, will you?"

The girl looked at the card, then glanced at him sharply; and what she felt somehow conveyed itself to the typists; there was a momentary pause in the startlingly swift tapping of the keys. One of the typists was a beauty in her way; with fluffy fair hair, china blue eyes, a white silk blouse which was meant to draw the male eye.

"I won't keep you a moment," the first girl said.

The china blue eyes were turned away.

Although there was only one door beyond the counter, it had the name *H. J. Netherby, London Manager,* on it. The girl disappeared, the door closed silently, and shut out all but a murmur of sound. In a moment the girl came back; all her movements had that brisk efficiency that the typists showed; and they were still working at furious speed.

"Mr. Netherby will be glad to see you, sir."

"Thank you."

Netherby was getting up from behind a large, flat topped desk. He sat with his back to the window, and to St. Paul's. In spite of that, his fresh complexion reminded Roger of Sol Riddle, but nothing else did. This man was red and round faced, small, unsmiling; he wasn't ugly, but he certainly wasn't handsome. He had the high colour, which looked almost fiery, of some florid man. He made no oiler to shake hands, but indicated a chair with his left hand.

Roger didn't notice anything odd, then.

"Thank you," he said. "Sorry to worry you, Mr. Netherby, but I've urgent and confidential business."

"I shall be glad to help," Netherby said, in a precise voice; he gave the impression of being a man who rehearsed everything carefully; who seldom acted without giving thought to what he was going to do and what its likely consequences would be. "Not that I can understand how I can be of assistance, Chief Inspector" – he glanced down at the card – "West."

"You employ a Mr. Michael Mallow, I believe."

In anyone else, the reaction might have been much more marked. In this man it was little more than a lift of very fair eyebrows, and a momentary gleam, perhaps of surprise, in the pale eyes.

"He is employed by my company, Mr. West. I simply take care of the London and southern business of the company. I might say, more exactly, that I supervise the orders which are obtained by our London and southern representatives. Mr. Michael Mallow represents us in a section of the south of England marked—if you will be good enough to turn your head—with the letter D."

Roger turned his head.

A map of the southern half of England was spread over much of the wall behind him. It was divided into about a dozen sections, each pastel washed a different colour, each with a large letter superimposed on it. That marked D was inside a segment starting from Croydon and widening as it reached the coast; Hoole was about the middle of the coastline it covered.

"In what way does Mr. Mallow interest Scotland Yard?" asked Netherby.

His expression and his tone were completely without emotion, almost without interest. In a curious way, his movements seemed laboured and stiff. Now Roger saw something which had missed him before.

Netherby's gloved right hand was resting on the desk, the fingers and thumb were crooked; the left was out of sight. The pose was so realistic that it deceived Roger at the first glance. The glove was of shiny black leather, without a wrinkle.

"You'll understand if I don't answer that directly," Roger said; he felt and sounded formal. Netherby probably had a machine like efficiency, but wasn't likely ever to become a man to know and to like. "I'll be grateful if you will tell me whether you know if Mr. Mallow has had any particular anxiety lately."

Netherby said: "I know of no personal trouble, unless you mean financial."

"I mean anything that affects him personally."

"Very well," said Netherby. "In that case, yes, I can give you a little confidential information." He paused. "I had asked Mr. Mallow to come and see me this morning, so as to give him an opportunity to explain certain peculiarities in his financial transactions with the company. He has chosen to ignore the invitation. It must be understood, of course, that anything I tell you is in complete confidence, and should not be regarded as in the nature of a formal charge until further information is forthcoming and the instructions of my Head Office have been received."

"That's understood."

What was coming next, Roger wondered. A serious charge, or a trifle? Netherby gave the impression that he would be as greatly concerned with an offence against the letter of the law as with a major crime. He had Mallow all sewn up and ready, and although he pretended to a certain reluctance, he probably derived an almost sadistic pleasure.

"Thank you. The matter is of some gravity, Mr. West. Certain inconsistencies in Mr. Mallow's order book have come to light. It is the custom of my company to assist its employees in every way possible. Some weeks ago Mr. Mallow asked for and obtained a substantial cash advance on commission due to him for sales made for future delivery during the past three months. Normally the commission would be paid quarterly; on this occasion the sum of a hundred and three pounds nine shillings was paid against commission supposedly due on fictitious—in fact, forged—orders."

Netherby paused, and moved his left hand an inch or two, almost as if it were feeling stiff.

"I had occasion to discuss the delivery of the order of one company, Morris & Son of Hoole, and discovered that the size of the order had been grossly exaggerated." Netherby gave a thin smile. "I use that word advisedly. The original order was for seventy five pounds worth of goods, the presented order was for one hundred and seventy five pounds worth. Having found proof of the one discrepancy, I checked on others, and have reason to suspect that there have been several. I have little doubt that evidence will be forthcoming. I imagine that a prosecution will be made, although, of course, I cannot prophesy the attitude of my company."

He stopped, still quite expressionless.

"How far back is the first alleged fraud?" Roger asked.

"Eighteen months, just prior to Christmas the year before last," said Netherby promptly.

"May I see the altered orders?"

"You may," said Netherby. "I have them in my drawer, under my personal supervision."

He leaned back, and so brought his other hand into view. He used it, working the finger and the thumb with slow, fascinating deliberation.

He handled a fat manila folder of papers without dexterity, but not clumsily; it was like watching a mechanical claw in action at the end of a man's arm.

Roger looked out of the window.

It was odd that he should be within sight of the searching police. It was somehow dispiriting to know that Mallow was now known to have been cheating his employers, although this was further evidence of Mallow's desperate financial plight. If Mallow had known of a hoard of stolen money—

"Here you are, Mr. West," Netherby said.

Roger looked through the orders. Some were probably genuine, others showed clearly, under a magnifying glass, that they had been altered. The Norris of Hoole order was more obvious than any.

"Do you know why the alteration in Norris's order is so large?" asked Roger. "It could hardly fail to be noticed."

Netherby showed his milk white teeth.

"It is not my duty to guess, Mr. West, but it may have something to do with the fact that Mallow is a friend of Norris, and may expect to be able to persuade him to keep quiet," Netherby said. "Are you satisfied now?"

"For the time being, yes." Roger stood up. "Thank you. May I take these orders?"

Netherby put a hand on the folder slowly, closed it, and said deliberately: "If you produce a written request from the proper authority, yes, Mr. West. Failing that, I must keep them at the disposal of my company."

Roger couldn't argue; and it really didn't matter whether he liked Netherby or not.

"I'll arrange the authority," he said.

He was already planning to go deeper into Mallow's defalcations here; a job for subordinates. Yet it all seemed unimportant, almost unreal. The urgent thing was to find Daphne Mallow—

To tell her what a rogue she'd married.

The police were working slowly out there among the ruins, giving no sign that they'd had results.

Chapter Seventeen

The Trail Of Michael Mallow

Roger West pulled up on one of the small plots of level ground, near the new catacombs, and got out; Wortleberry squeezed himself out on the other side. He looked hot; thick grey Harris tweeds weren't right for the day. He kept wiping his forehead, too, and then looked up at St. Paul's as if he couldn't believe that he was actually standing within a stone's throw of it.

Roger left his radio switched on, and a man near it. They walked precariously towards the spot where a group of police were searching. There were more than the previous night; firemen were helping, too. No one knew that the spot they sought was a hundred yards from the nearer group; a spot in the shadow of a wall which they might reach today if they kept going at the same pace.

Two or three boys were climbing over the walls in the distance, kicking up dust, standing every now and again and watching the police. They were scornfully oblivious of the danger sign. One of them started to throw stones at a little remnant of a wall which stuck up like a stump of a tooth in an octogenarian's mouth. The rattling sound as the stones pitched came clearly. The police took no notice, except at a distance, and the boys didn't venture too close.

Newspaper men did; there were half a dozen of them, and they came hurrying when they spotted Roger.

"'Morning, Handsome."

"Got anything for us?"

"That true, Mallow's been released?"

"Seriously think his wife's here, Handsome?"

Roger seized on that one.

"We know she was here last night, she hasn't been seen to leave, and we're not taking any chances. But we know Ginn's dangerous, too. He might have had a chance to get away before all the publicity, but now he knows he hasn't."

"He's the type who'll die fighting in a corner, isn't he?" a man asked.

"Could be."

"Can we quote you?"

"No."

"You don't think he'll get away?"

"He can't get away. All the ports, airfields, and stations are being watched. Every police station and every newspaper in the country will have a copy of his photograph before the day's out. His will be on television tonight; so will Mrs. Mallow's. We're using everything we've got to find Mrs. Mallow."

"Think he'll do her more harm?"

"It's an obvious risk."

"Think she's dead?"

"I just hope not."

"Pretty free with your spiel this morning, Handsome, aren't you?" one of the men asked, grinning.

"When publicity will help, I'm all for publicity!" Roger grinned back. He looked better, because he was active again; and Wortleberry had helped. Mallow's release was another cause for hope; and the chief one was that he would find Mrs. Mallow alive. "Here's something off the record," he added, and didn't trouble to emphasise that it was "off"; they would respect it. "Superintendent Wortleberry of the Hoole Constabulary found the rock with which a man at Hoole was probably battered to death."

Six pairs of eyes switched to Wortleberry.

Roger was half sorry he'd said it, but then had a surprise. Wortleberry positively glowed. He was good with the Press, too;

mild, almost benign, friendly. What was more, he enjoyed his impromptu Press conference.

Roger stifled a laugh.

The man by his car signalled.

He left Wortleberry to the Fleet Street men, and hurried back.

"Radio for you, sir."

"Thanks." There was always the hope that it would be really big news. He grabbed the receiver. "West speaking."

"Two flashes, Mr. West," said a man in the Information Room at the Yard. "First, a message from Bradding, down at Hoole. He's found several reddish human hairs on the corner of an oak beam at Reedon's cottage—a beam at the half landing, the report says. They're longish hairs, four or five inches, and curly. A man's, almost for certain, very coarse."

"Red hair," Roger echoed. "Good, thanks. What's next?"

"Report from Appleby, sir, who's following Michael Mallow. When Mallow turned into Parliament Street, a newsboy—middle aged chap, sir—got up and followed him to Trafalgar Square. Then Mallow went to a telephone. So did the other man. Both made calls, one from a public box, one from a tobacconist's. The newsboy's still following Mallow, sir. Appleby is following both, and Oddy's covering. Oddy passed this on through a man on the beat, sir."

"Fine. Which way are they heading?"

"For the City, sir."

"Could be the East End," Roger remarked. "Walking, or by bus?"

"Walking, sir."

"Thanks," Roger said, and rang off.

He felt a simmering of excitement based on new hope. Why had Mallow telephoned anyone so quickly – and who? He must know that he was being watched; and Ginn would realise that he would be, too.

That drove Roger back to the basic question: why had Ginn been so anxious to have Mallow free? Which really meant, why was Ginn so sure that Mallow had the stolen money?

Roger went over Mallow's story item by item; then over the known facts, including the fifty one pounds which had been sent to

Daphne Mallow anonymously, and in an envelope with that unidentified man's finger prints.

There were the coarse red hairs. He had a hazy picture of a man with red hair, somewhere in this case. If he worried over it too much, he'd only irritate himself and probably drive the recollection farther away. He put it out of his mind.

Had Mallow telephoned Ginn, offering a deal?

Was the man who had followed Mallow one of Ginn's men? He might be, but it was also as possible that he was a Fleet Street man; there were at least three who would enter into the spirit of a job thoroughly enough to pose as newspaper sellers.

He ought to go back to the office. There were a hundred things he might be doing. This wasn't the only case, and this wasn't the only angle. But he didn't want to go. He stood looking on at the slow, deliberate pace of the searching police. Wortleberry was still with the newspapermen, but they were no longer talking. The three boys, not yet in their teens and probably playing truant, were still running about the rubble, occasionally hurling stones at the empty windows of the wall marked danger. It was astonishing how often the stones soared through; only occasionally did they smack against the wall.

Roger joined Wortleberry.

"Know of a man with red hair in this case?" he asked. "A friend of Reedon's or a friend of Mallow."

"Eh? Red hair?"

Wortleberry, not expecting the question, needed time to think.

"Fairly long hair for a man, very coarse."

"Well, hm, yes, I should think so," Wortleberry said calmly. "Pal of both of 'em, if it comes to that. Man named Norris, rather a big fellow, with—" Wortleberry broke off, gasping.

Roger waited for it.

"*Big fellow with big hands*," breathed Wortleberry. "Biggest hands I've ever seen on a man. Got a grip like an elephant's trunk. Ben *Norris*. Gor' this is a turn up—"

He broke off again, and then looked almost ludicrous. "Where's he come in, then?"

"Red hairs at the cottage."

"Gor'," breathed Wortleberry. "Can I speak to my office on that radio thing?" He was already lumbering back towards the car. "They could pick up a set of his dabs."

"Speak to the Yard, they'll send your message."

Roger nicked on the walkie talkie, and Wortleberry, leaning into the car with his great posterior still outside, picked up the receiver and proceeded to give absolute and precise instructions.

"Ask my chaps at Hoole to go and see Benjamin Norris, in the High Street. Ask him where he was on Friday night. All friendly. Just get his answers. Set of his prints, too. Let me know at the Yard, please." He put the walkie talkie down quickly, almost as if he were afraid that it would shock him. "That all right?" he asked. "Thanks."

"Tell me more about Norris," urged Roger.

"Runs a wholesale stationery and office equipment business," Wortleberry said. "Good customer of Mallow's, too, they've been friends ever since they came to live in Hoole. Not a good type, though, talks all the time—when I knew Mallow was friendly with him I started to have doubts about Mallow. Better get back to the Yard, hadn't we?" Wortleberry asked, and then gave a shy grin. "Truth about me is, I'm not happy if I haven't got a comfortable chair and a telephone handy."

"We'll get straight back," Roger promised.

He didn't explain that a man named Norris, with a stationery and office equipment shop in Hoole, had provided the key evidence of Mallow's frauds.

They got into the car, and he was about to turn left when he saw that a big van was holding up traffic in the one way street leading to Ludgate Hill. He went along another narrow road, and then turned right, towards Holborn and the shored up shells of buildings.

He passed the stone throwing boys, the unsafe walls, and within fifty yards of Daphne Mallow, who was a crumpled heap on the floor of that dark hole; the scarf tight, her breathing shallow, her pulse very slow.

They'd been back at the Yard for ten minutes when a message came from Hoole.

Norris had travelled up to London on the six thirty train for the previous evening, and had stayed the night; he'd not told anyone where he would be.

He was still away, and hadn't sent a message.

Of course – a red haired man, talking to Daphne Mallow on the platform!

The red haired man named Norris, moving his big, bulky figure very fast, went into an empty house at Clapham Common, with an order to view in his possession. He was not interested in the house as a proposition, but in Lefty Ginn, who was to meet him there.

Ginn was already waiting.

He stood erect and grim, with his flabby, grey yellow face looking very unhealthy, his eyes narrowed as if light hurt them. He had one hand in his trousers pocket, a half smoked cigarette in the other.

Norris began to talk.

"Listen, Lefty, what's the game? Why d'you come out into the open, asking for trouble, isn't it? Why don't you lie low, and let me—"

"Shut up," Ginn said.

"But Lefty, it's asking for trouble, and—"

"You're asking for trouble," Ginn said in his hard, grating voice. "Mallow isn't out yet, but I think he will be. He's bound to 'phone you for help. You meet him, and make him talk. Got it?"

"But we could have fixed all this by telephone, Lefty! I don't see why—" The spate of words came swiftly, always in full flood.

"I wanted you to understand I won't take any double crossing, from you or anyone," Ginn said.

"Me? Double cross *you*?" Norris gave a nervous laugh. "Wouldn't dare to, Lefty, wouldn't want to, anyway."

"You've got a chance to prove how loyal you are. Make him hand over the dough."

Norris gasped: "I can't make him! If he won't—"

"If you can't get it, bring him here."

Norris spluttered, but didn't argue.

When he went off, he kept looking round at Ginn. It was almost as if Ginn suspected that he, not Mallow, had taken the money.

Norris didn't feel at all good, but somehow he would have to bring Mallow here, he daren't fail Ginn.

The messages from Detective Sergeant Appleby, an astute, self effacing man whose genius for following suspects without being suspected had helped to keep him down to sergeant's rank for over twenty years, came in over a period of two hours and nine minutes. They reached the Yard by devious means; some Appleby telephoned himself; two came through patrol cars which he stopped, and which flashed radiotelephone messages to the Yard; two came from policemen on duty whom he or Oddy stopped. One came through the conductor of a bus on which Mallow travelled, with Appleby a few seats behind him.

The most significant reached Roger on buff memorandum forms on which all Yard messages were relayed throughout the building.

11.58. After leaving the Yard Mallow went to Parliament Street. From a cafe on a corner of Cannon Row, he was followed by a small man, name not known, who was obviously interested in him. Mallow turned towards Trafalgar Square.

12.21. Near Trafalgar Square the small man who had followed Mallow caught up with him and spoke. I was too far away to overhear any part of the conversation. Mallow appeared to be angry. The other man left him. I decided not to send Oddy to follow this individual, but to make sure that we didn't lose Mallow. Description of short man follows . . .

Once the description was out, it was flashed to all police stations; but it was so nondescript that no one expected results.

12.48. Mallow, still obviously greatly agitated, is on top deck of a Number 15 bus, heading towards the City and Aldgate. I am on lower deck. Oddy is following in a taxi.

1.14. Mallow is approaching a small cafe at the corner of Widclaw Street, Whitechapel. He now appears to suspect that he is being followed. I have accordingly fallen back, and Oddy is now closer to Mallow.

1.26. Mallow has been in the cafe for ten minutes, sitting at a table on his own, without ordering food or drink. He appears to have told a waitress that he is waiting for a companion.

1.34. A big, red haired man dressed in a pin stripe brown suit is now sitting with Mallow at the cafe, and both men have given an order. They appear to be on bad terms.

1.59. Mallow and the red haired man have left the cafe together, and, still on bad terms, have hired a taxi and are about to get in. Taxi is a blue Beardmore, pre war, registration number 8V234. Am following. Have requested nearby patrol car to follow also.

2.27. Mallow and red haired man now walking across Clapham Common. Mallow looks acutely distressed. The men are not speaking to each other. Have requested a Divisional Sergeant to have local men watch Mallow and his companion.

2.40. Mallow and his companion have entered the grounds of a private house which has a "For Sale" board up in the front garden. A wall and overgrown bushes hide the lower part of the house from sight. Am endeavouring to maintain close observation from a neighbouring house.

2.49. Mallow has left the house, alone, looking extremely agitated. I am following.

2.54. Red haired man has been found in grounds of the house, with the back of his head smashed in. Death appears to have been instantaneous.

2.59. Mallow has been detained and is being brought to the Yard for questioning.

Mallow's appearance had been bad enough before; it was dreadful now. His eyes looked as if it hurt to keep them open. His aggressiveness only spurted up occasionally.

He was in the charge room at Cannon Row, with Roger, Wortleberry, and a Yard sergeant. It was now nearly four o'clock. There had been no news of Ginn, and none of Mallow's wife, none of the man who had followed Mallow from Parliament Street. They knew, now, that the dead man was Ben Norris of Hoole; Wortleberry hadn't needed a second glance.

Norris's fingers were very big and flat; his prints had been at Reedon's cottage, and on the envelope in which the fifty one pounds had been sent to Mallow's wife.

"Do you think I don't know what's going to happen?" Mallow said, in a choky voice. "I'm going to be tried for murder, and found guilty, and hanged. But I didn't kill him. I haven't killed anyone. Ben said he had news of Daff, and wanted to meet me at this cafe in Whitechapel. I had to go, I had to. For Daff—"

Roger said quietly: "How did he get in touch with you?"

"I telephoned him at his hotel."

"How did you know where he was staying?"

"I knew he was coming to London this week, he always stays at the same hotel, out at Cromwell Road. I wanted to borrow some money. He said he'd see what he could do, and told me where to meet him."

There was a long, edgy pause; and then Roger changed the whole tempo, voice, eyes, manner, seemed to join in the eruption.

"You're lying, as you've lied all the time," he said roughly. "You killed Norris."

"I didn't! I swear—"

"He knew you killed Reedon, so you lured him there and smashed his skull to pieces."

"It's a lie!" screeched Mallow.

"You'll be hanged for it if you don't tell us why you bolted from Reedon's cottage. Come on, out with it."

There was another pause, so taut it was like a balloon being blown up bigger and bigger.

Then: "You'll never believe me!"

"Try us."

"It's a waste of time."

"You've got plenty, before you hang."

"You've judged me already, you think I'm guilty."

"I don't give a damn whether you're guilty or not. I want to find your wife."

That pulled Mallow up sharply; the hissing intake of his breath was like the escape of steam from a tight valve.

"That—that's your job, you've got to find her."

"To find her, we've got to find Ginn. Where is he?"

"I don't know. I'd never heard of him until yesterday. I swear—"

"Save your breath. Where can we find Ginn?"

"I don't know!"

"If I had my way, I'd use the cat on you until you were raw," growled Roger. "Remember your wife? She's a nice girl. Pretty, nice figure, everything that—"

"Shut up!"

"Where's Ginn?"

"*I don't know!*"

"He'll kill her."

"I don't know where he is. Can't you—can't you see what happened?" Mallow sobbed. "Ben Norris said he could help, Ginn must have found out we were going to meet, and gone and killed him. I've been framed again, I—" He stopped.

The silence was like the hush after a clash of cymbals. Mallow backed away, slowly. Roger eyed him with a steady, accusing stare.

The sergeant looked up from his notes. Wortleberry rumbled and shifted his feet.

"So Ginn was going to frame you *again*," said Roger softly. "When was the first time?"

Mallow didn't answer.

Roger rasped: "So that's how fond you are of your wife. Let Ginn have her, and do what he likes with her. Reward for love."

"Don't!" gasped Mallow.

"She loves, and she trusted you."

"Don't keep talking about my wife!"

"Where's that photograph of her, Super?" asked Roger. "The coloured one. Did I give it to you?"

Wortleberry began to feel in his breast pocket.

Mallow choked: "I—I don't know where Ginn is, I swear I don't. That's why I wanted to—to see Norris. To find out, and go to Ginn. I've never—I've never met Ginn. Honest to God, I haven't. It—it was Norris who—who framed me. He knew Ginn."

Roger had relaxed, and was offering cigarettes. Mallow took one, broke in his hoarse story for a light, and went on, more chokily than ever: "I—I'll tell you what happened, everything. It's—it's my own crazy fault, if I hadn't put so much on the gees—well, I did." He looked about to collapse, and Roger pushed a chair up; he dropped on to it. "I needed some money, I'd got into debt. I—I told Norris. He put me up to—to a few wrinkles. Getting commission in advance, fake orders, things like that. I thought I'd win my money back, I didn't mean—" He broke off; there were tears in his eyes.

Roger waited.

"I just couldn't get out of debt," Mallow went on. "I'd borrowed a hell of a lot from Tony Reedon, hadn't the nerve to ask for more. Then—then Norris told me he'd get me some if I'd help him. I was to ask Reedon for more, to—to go and see him at the cottage on—on Friday night. Midnight."

Roger still didn't speak.

"I didn't know why," Mallow went on, "but—but I had to. Norris said he'd tell the firm about those forged orders if I didn't. So I went there. Someone hit me, before I got to the cottage. I—I went out, like a light." He licked his lips, and was silent for several seconds; it seemed like minutes. "When—when I came round, the lights were on in the cottage, and—and I went to see what was—was up. I thought there'd been—been a burglary. I went in, and there was a— a man coming down the stairs. Big man, with—with a sack. Green sack, like—like sacks for registered letters." He licked his lips again, noisily. "He—he pulled a knife. I went for him, there was—was a ghastly struggle, and I—I would have killed him, if I could, but—but I didn't."

"Who did?" Roger asked quietly.

"I swear I don't know. Someone crept up behind me, and hit me over the head. I went out again, and—and when I came round, there—there he was."

"The same man?"

"Yes."

"Dead?"

"Yes, he—his head was smashed in."

"See anyone else?"

"No."

"Norris?"

"No one."

"The green bag?"

"It was gone."

"See Reedon?"

"*No!*"

There was another pause. In it, Roger took a whisky flask from his hip pocket, and offered it. Mallow first looked as if he couldn't believe his eyes, and then grabbed.

He gulped whisky down.

"Easy," said Roger, and took the flask. "Why didn't you go to the police?"

Mallow didn't answer.

"Let's have it all, Mallow."

"I—I didn't think anyone would believe me."

"You mean, you hoped no one would know you'd been to the cottage. That it?"

"I—"

"Is that it?"

"Yes," muttered Mallow. "I was crazy with fear. Crazy. I came up here, and phoned Norris. He said he'd come to town, told me where he'd be staying; that's really how I knew where to phone him."

"What did he say?"

"He said—he said Ginn wanted the money." Mallow stretched out trembling hands, and looked into Roger's face. "I don't know anything about the money. Norris said it was in the green bag. Money and jewels, from an old robbery. He said Tony Reedon was really a crook named Rawson, who'd pulled off a big haul and—and kept it in the cottage. Norris said Ginn was after it, Ginn knew about the burglary years ago, but Rawson disappeared. Then he—*Norris, the swine*—recognised Tony. Norris used to be a fence, a—you know. He told Ginn, Ginn planned the raid on the cottage. I—I'm pretty sure they wanted me there to—to kill Tony and frame me."

There was another pause.

"Did you *know* that Reedon was dead then?" Roger asked softly.

"No! Don't twist everything I say. Norris told me he was, I put two and two together."

There was a long pause, while Roger considered. This might be true; there was no way of telling.

Roger said quietly: "This man coming down the stairs, the man you say was killed while you were knocked out. Did you know him?"

"No."

"Did you see anyone else?"

"I've told you—no."

"Mallow, did you kill that man?"

"I swear I didn't," cried Mallow, and he began to sob.

There wasn't much more to get out of him. Between gasps and sobs, he said that he'd slept in his car the first night, and in a third rate hotel the following night, all the time terrified of being recognised. He gave the name of the hotel, and the name he had used: White.

That was all.

"We've never had more evidence on a man," Roger said roughly. "Short of catching him red handed, we couldn't have a stronger case. The hell of it is, I don't feel sure that he's lying. But if we don't uncover a lot more evidence, he'll hang. And his wife—" He broke off.

"What about the search near St. Paul's?" asked Chatworth. "Calling it off?"

"Every possible spot will have been searched by nightfall," Roger said. "I'd rather wait until then before stopping it."

"I'm not so sure," Chatworth said, without enthusiasm. "It will be a remarkable thing if she's in the last place you look. But I know, I know, you have to be thorough. What about this man Norris— know anything more about him?"

"He was certainly at the cottage when Chips Silver was murdered," Roger said. "The red hairs were his, we've proved that. Wortleberry's checking where he can, but Norris had no record. All we know is that he and Ginn were at the cottage. It looks as if they might have planned to frame Mallow for Reedon's murder, but the mystery is in the missing green bag. If Norris stole it, and Ginn thinks that Mallow did, then Ginn—" He broke off. "The man who followed Mallow today was Abbey, of the *Echo*," he declared abruptly. "The only man we're still after is Ginn himself. The East End's been turned upside down, and there isn't a whisper of any kind. It's almost as if the swine had never existed. The only two people who knew him really well are dead—Chips Silver and Gladys Domwell. He's been going in and out of the country for years, may be on board a ship that's hours out at sea. We've broadcast his description to all ships which he might be on, but we'll be lucky if that leads anywhere. If we don't find Ginn, I think we'll hang Mallow—although I'm not sure that he's a killer. And if we don't find Ginn, we may never find Mallow's wife."

Chatworth didn't speak.

Roger said: 'We're going all out on Norris, and we'll check Mallow's movements again. If we could only find the stuff, we would get headlines in the Press. Ginn might ease off the girl if he knew we've got the goods."

"Couldn't we pretend—" began Chatworth.

"Before we could convince Ginn that we had the bag, we'd have to be able to give the Press a description of its contents," Roger said simply. "We can't, until we find it."

They could not find the green bag – at Norris's hotel, at Mallow's, or anywhere. They searched for cloakroom tickets, safe deposit keys, any evidence of a hiding place, and they found none.

They did find that a photograph of Reedon, taken some years ago, tallied with one of a youth named Rawson, locksmith apprentice who had once been suspected of a part in a major robbery, and had afterwards disappeared.

Chapter Eighteen

The Wall

Wortleberry snuffled and grunted as he sat in the car next to Roger, kept looking at Roger's set face, gulping, staring at the massed traffic ahead, then looking back at Roger. They were near the end of Blackfriars Bridge when at last he said what was on his mind.

"If only I'd suspected Norris—"

"No one did, no one had any reason to," Roger said.

There was a gap in the traffic; he put the car into it, and Wortleberry's head bobbed forward; so he swallowed his words and, settling down, looked even more ill at ease.

They just beat the lights.

Roger stared straight ahead.

"You worry too much," he said, "and you're one of the few country cops I haven't wished back in their own nice cosy offices." His tone didn't match the words, but he tried to make it. "Think Mallow was lying?"

"Could be," said Wortleberry. "It's a hell of a good story."

"Prints prove that Ginn and Norris were both there," Roger said.

"Some crooks never learn, and always leave their dabs," Wortleberry said. "Smart ones, too."

Up to a point, that was true.

"You've taken to Mallow, haven't you?" Wortleberry went on.

"Wouldn't say that." They were at Ludgate Circus, and a glance to the right showed the great dome; massed pale granite with the

162

sun shining on the cross which crowned it. "I just have a nasty feeling that he may be telling the truth. There's a hell of a lot of room for doubt."

Roger turned off the main road, and was soon parked near the main body of police cars. The little groups of men, police as well as firemen, were still dotted about. Fifty or sixty idlers were watching, with the intentness which the empty minded often showed in a hole in the road.

Newspapermen came up to Roger.

"That true you're calling it off, Handsome?" one man asked.

"Anything in the rumour that Ginn's got out of the country?" a second inquired smoothly.

"What's this about another murder, Handsome?"

"Gentlemen," said Roger, as nearly sarcastic as he would let himself be with the Press, "the answer to the middle one is that the police don't listen to rumour; to the last, yes, there has been another murder—read the newspapers to find out all about it. As for calling it all off—"

"Are you?" two insisted.

The bleakness came back. The futility of looking for anyone amid this desolation, now that one search had failed, swept over Roger. No matter which way he looked, there wasn't much in it for him. If Daphne Mallow were near here, she was probably dead or dying. The day might come, in a year or in ten years, when they got round to building again and putting in new foundations, when they'd find her skeleton. If she weren't here – the laugh was on him.

He'd no proof at all that she had been here for more than a few minutes.

The nearest newspaperman was very short, with a button nose and button eyes; an aggressive little terrier of a man.

"Give us a break, Handsome. Are you calling it off?"

Roger looked at him bleakly.

"Yes," he said. "Within the next hour."

He hardly knew why he added "the next hour". He'd no authority; just Chatworth's instructions to call it off, given less than an hour ago. He would search on, while daylight lasted and through tomorrow, if he had his way; but Authority had spoken. He didn't hide the fact that he disagreed with the verdict, but no one referred to that. Wortleberry pushed his hands deep in his baggy pockets.

Two minutes later, when his mood was at its worst, Roger saw a huge uniformed policeman coming towards him, with a small boy at his side. They were hand in hand. The boy was probably average size, but the policeman made him into a Lilliputian; at any other time it would have been comical.

The boy was one of those who had been throwing stones. He had the sharp features and the keen eyes of the Cockney; a fine natural quiff of hair; clothes which needed the needle; a face which needed washing. He couldn't be more than eleven or twelve, but had the forced maturity of a youth twice his years. Yet he was ill at ease.

Why bring a kid along for some silly misdemeanour, Roger wondered irritably; some of these damned flatfoots behaved as if they'd never had a kid of their own. This one's right ear stuck out more than his left.

The constable came ponderously to a standstill.

"Chief Inspector West, sir?"

Roger said, "Yes," and tried to find a grin for the boy; it wouldn't come.

"This lad has an interesting statement to make, sir."

Roger thought savagely: "I'm getting dull witted."

He hadn't even seen this ill assorted pair as heralds of hope, and slid out of the mood of despondency with the unthinking speed of a thirsty man who sees water.

"Has he, then. What's this about, son?" There was no difficulty in his grin, now; Martin and Richard would have recognised it. "Found some stolen loot?"

He won a responding grin.

"Loot, nothing," the boy said. He hadn't a nasal accent, barely a hint of Cockney. "I asked the copper what you're all looking for, he told me about this cove, Ginn."

"I considered that advisable," said the constable, speaking as he would write his report.

"Seen him?" asked Roger.

"I don't say I have, I don't say I haven't," answered the boy, "but I *might* have, mister. Over there." He pointed towards the high wall, with the sign which so clearly said danger. "Two or three times I seen him, when it's getting late. I can show you the door he goes through, if it's the chap."

"*Door?*"

"He states," announced the policeman, "that he has seen this person climb down into one of the basements that was, and pull open a door in a corner."

"What are we waiting for?" Roger demanded sharply, and started off. "What's your name, George?"

"Nark it," the boy said. "You know." He grinned again. "Seen this guy several times—had a moll with him, sometimes."

They were hurrying, and drawing nearer that brooding wall. Nothing suggested that it was as dangerous as that notice said; it stood sheer and tall, darkened by weather, flames, and smoke, with the empty window frames letting through the light of day. Huge wooden beams which shored it up seemed strong enough to hold it for another fifty years.

"What do you mean, moll?" Roger demanded, but he wasn't thinking of keeping the youngster at ease, only about this door in the wall of a basement. He didn't give the big wall a thought.

"*You* know. Dame, peach, skirt, *moll.*"

"I'll 'moll' you," Roger said. "Nip ahead and show me the spot, will you?"

The big policeman and Wortleberry were following; so were two newspapermen, including the little chap with the button eyes and button nose; an odd procession. Elsewhere, the police worked at the same steady pace, and the watchers gazed without knowing what was going on. Roger and the boy came within the shadow of the wall, and the boy reached the place where Ginn and Gladys had climbed up from the basement; he nipped down, and disappeared from sight.

When Roger reached the edge, the boy was at the far corner.

That was the first sharp disappointment, for it looked just like a part of the rest of the basement wall; made of brick, not at all like a door. Roger hesitated. The police and the pressmen were twenty yards behind. The boy nipped across round and beckoned, then began to prise at the wall with a piece of stiff wire; he was certainly in earnest, even if he'd made a mistake in the actual spot.

"You sure that's the place?" Roger called, as he jumped down.

" 'Course I'm sure, seen it open often enough," said the boy scornfully. "Tried to get in, too, but never managed it. I think he has a key. This brick's a bit loose, see."

He was poking the wire beside the brick, and the brick actually moved.

Roger's heart jumped.

"Fine! Let me—"

"*Got it*," breathed the boy, and then pulled the loose brick out.

He pulled too quickly, and it dropped and fell on his toe. At any other time his language would have shaken the hardest bitten Yard man, but Roger wasn't thinking about a schoolboy's profanity, only of the gap in the wall.

Beyond, was a keyhole.

It wasn't going to be easy to get at that keyhole with a pick lock. Obviously the bricks were built on the outside of a steel door; probably this had once been a vault, possibly beneath a bank. That didn't matter; what mattered was getting at the door.

"Get someone with pick axes," Roger called. "Hurry!"

He glanced swiftly round, and caught sight of the boy, darting to the right. The boy's fingers closed round a broken piece of iron girder, some two feet long and twisted in the heat of the fire.

"This do, sir?"

Sir.

"Fine, George. What is—?" Roger didn't finish the question, but jumped out of the way, for the lad raised the broken girder in his two lean hands, then brought it down at the wall with all the strength he could muster.

The eagerness on the young face was unbelievable; Roger hadn't the heart to stop him, and let him bring it down three times – a rain of blows far less puny than seemed likely.

No one noticed that the tremors ran along from the ground to the high wall.

No one noticed the wall trembling.

"Let me," Roger said. He didn't use his full strength, but levered at several bricks near the keyhole; the lad had loosened them, and they came out with trouble. "That's fine. You did the work, I get the pickings! Ever seen a pick lock?"

"You mean *skeleton* key?"

"That's right."

"But you're a copper!"

Roger grinned, lively as the boy.

"That's right, too!"

He stopped speaking, because of the onrush of excitement. This couldn't be coincidence, could it? The boy had really seen Ginn, if Daphne Mallow were anywhere here she would be behind this door. He had to take it carefully – more haste less speed. Old saw! The boy's gaze was tense and taut, like a physical thing. Roger's hands moved, he felt the key get a grip and began to turn firmly.

He heard a sound which seemed to come from a long way off; a kind of crunching, followed by a loud crack. He took no notice, although he heard a man say sharply: "What's that?" Two policemen were jumping down into the basement, then turned to pick up pick axes; one newspaperman was half way between the edge and Roger and the boy.

All of these looked round, startled.

The lock clicked back.

"Got it!" breathed Roger. "Lend a hand, George, pull like the very devil."

He gripped a brick on one side of the hole; the boy gripped another. They pulled with all their weight, desperately. The door began to open, and yielded up its darkness. The unfamiliar, grinding and cracking noise came from behind, a shadow seemed to be moving over them slowly and remorselessly.

Wortleberry bellowed in a voice which blasted the rending, ominous noises.

"*Get away, Handsome! Wall's falling!*"

Roger heard; and in a moment of frightening clarity understood what the noises were. The boy realised it, too. They turned round, moving in jerks, like running down clockwork toys. The great dark wall towered above them at a monstrous height; and was falling slowly, falling so that loose pieces fell from the top and crashed into the basement.

There was no hope for anyone in the basement. The newspaperman and the two policemen were rushing madly away, arms folded above their heads in almost pathetic gesture of defence.

The boy was petrified as he watched the wall falling faster and faster.

Something cracked inside Roger. He grabbed the boy and thrust him into the darkness beyond the door, squeezed through, jumped into the black void, banged into the boy and grabbed him.

Then all light was cut off as the avalanche of brick fell against the door, slamming it. A crack as of thunder was followed by a deafening, frightening roar. The earth trembled and the unseen walls shook.

Chapter Nineteen

The Cupboard

The avalanche of sound had ceased. Man and boy stood together, closely, as if they were father and son, the boy's arms tight round Roger's waist, his face buried against Roger's coat. Dust, shaken up by the impact, rose in choking clouds and made it difficult to breathe. It stung the eyes and made it easy to think that they would suffocate, that there was no hope of breathing fresh air, or of breathing at all for long. Roger struggled for breath, and fought his own fear; and he must also fight the boy's.

It was all quiet, now; there was just the choking dust.

He eased the boy away.

"It's all right," he said. "This wall held. Our lucky day." It wasn't easy to speak, he paused between every two or three words, and his voice sounded strange even on his own ears. The lad still gripped him – his hand, now that he couldn't encircle his waist. "Let me have my hand back," Roger managed to say, "then I can get a light."

The boy snatched his hands away, desperately eager for a light. He was much more help than hindrance, for he forced calmness to Roger; the moment of panic had already passed. The dust was just dust, unpleasant but not deadly, and they could breathe.

Roger took out his lighter.

"I filled it last night," he said, "we're all right for a bit. It won't be long before they dig us out." Reason told him that men outside were already starting; and reason told him that there were others to dig for besides him and the boy. He thought of Wortleberry, who might have been struck down. "Half a mo'."

He flicked the lighter.

The small yellow light was so strong at first that it dazzled them both. He caught a glimpse of the youngster's face smeared with dust, and then it vanished; he could see the brightness of the boy's eyes as he might see the filament of a lamp after staring at it.

He opened his eyes narrowly.

The swirling dust was not thick enough to prevent them from looking about; and the boy was as eager as Roger.

There, on the box which served as a table, was a candle in the neck of a beer bottle. Strictly speaking, half a candle, with the wax set hard on the outside of the bottle and looking like a tiny frozen waterfall. Roger's hand wasn't steady, and the boy's voice shook.

"L—l—look, someone—someone *lives* here."

Roger gritted his teeth as he went forward and lit the candle. The wick caught very slowly, the dust sparked, the lighter went out; just a tiny little ball of yellow light remained, with the dust swirling about it, as if intent on putting it out.

Then the candle flame grew larger.

He had to have light, but mustn't keep it for long; they would need every precious bit of oxygen, and the open flame would burn it too quickly.

They looked about them, seeing the bed in the corner, the pin up photographs, the oddments of food, the chair – and the door of the cupboard in the corner.

And on Daphne Mallow's suitcase, with its bright red corners.

Roger stared at it.

After a long pause, the boy said: "What—what's the matter?"

"Er—reaction, I expect," Roger made himself say. "Bit of a shock for us both, wasn't it, Geo—what *is* your name?"

"Stop kidding," the boy said.

That made Roger stop to think about him at a time when he didn't want to. He wanted to face the ugly fact that there was no sign of Daphne Mallow, only the suitcase and the closed cupboard door. He wanted to open the door, and search thoroughly. He had honestly forgotten that they were buried here; and his manner had eased the boy's fears.

"See if you can get that suitcase open," he said, almost roughly. "I'll try that door."

He went forward; and it was hard to say why he went so slowly; or seemed to. He was suffering from shock more than he had realised. He saw the boy move towards the suitcase, and bend down. He saw the odd pieces of shiny leather, and the glove mould. He ignored that as he went to the door, gripped the metal handle, turned, and pulled. If it were locked …

It opened.

His shadow was cast over Daphne Mallow, where she lay in a heap on the floor.

He stood utterly still.

"*Blimey!*" breathed the boy, "a bloody corpse!"

She was alive.

She lay on the blanket bed, now, belt loosened, shoes off, clothes piled up on her. Her pulse was very faint. It was impossible to judge how long she would survive unless she had medical help. The air here was foul, even now that the dust had settled. Her mouth and lips were raw and sore from the scarf which Roger had cut away. Her wrists were badly chafed by the cord.

Would they be here for hours or for a day?

How long could she stay alive?

With the gentle candlelight shining upon her, something of her beauty showed, although her sore lips were slack and her forehead lined and her eyes had great dark shadows beneath them. It was hard to believe that she was breathing.

The boy asked hoarsely: "Is she going to peg out, mister?"

"Not if we can save her," Roger said.

It was then exactly five o'clock. The illuminated dial of his watch wasn't damaged, they would be able to see the time in the dark. The candle wouldn't last long – it mustn't be allowed to burn much longer, anyhow. Suddenly, he found himself moving away from

JOHN CREASEY

Daphne Mallow as she clung to life. He had a lot of other problems.
How to keep alive, for one thing, and give their rescuers a chance.

"Listen, George," he said, and then stopped arid stared into the
bright eyes, and put his head on one side. "This time I mean to have
an answer," he said firmly, "no fooling. What *is* your name?"

The boy said: "Stop kid—"

Roger gripped the jutting ear.

"Come on, let's have it."

"But you know it!" the boy squealed. "It's George—George
Smith. Why, you keep calling me George!"

Roger let him go.

It was impossible not to laugh, although the sound was more like
a giggle. That did him good. He lost another two minutes, getting
on top of himself, and then began to treat George Smith as he
would have treated Martin or Richard, in like circumstances; as he
would an adult.

"Now, listen. We don't know how long we're going to be here. It
may be for several hours. It's a small room, and pretty stuffy
already—and no fresh air's coming in: follow me?"

"Could die from lack of oxygen," George said promptly. "Like
they nearly did on Everest."

Roger blessed him.

"That's right. But if we do everything slowly, we'll conserve the
oxygen. The way to make it last longest would be to go to sleep, but
there are several things to do first—but slowly, see. Don't rush
about. Okay?"

"Okay."

"Fine. Look round for more candles, matches, and food, will you?
There's a kettle over there, and a bucket—see how we're fixed. I've
got a job to do too—must find traces of Ginn, and see if he's left
anything here."

"You mean, jewels or something?" George was eager.

"Could be."

"Blimey," George breathed again.

He would be all right for a little while, but the first hour wasn't
the problem for any of them; not even for the unconscious woman.

172

If there were some sound from outside, some indication that men were working already, it would help; there couldn't be so many tons of stuff in one wall, could there?

Both moved very slowly.

Roger found more pieces of leather – mostly black glacé kid, but there was some pigskin and some plain brown glove leather. Apparently Gladys Domwell had done quite a lot of work here, too; that was one way to show your love for a man. And he'd killed her as callously as he would kill a rabbit. Roger could remember the little frightened squeal, then the falling of her body. He tried to shut both out of his mind.

He could hear George busy with water, and smelt methylated spirits; he glanced across at the corner, where the boy was holding up a bottle. One problem was to keep the boy moving at half speed.

"Got a spirit stove and plenty of water, some grub, too, we can hold out for days," George whispered almost scornfully; for the moment, apparently, he had forgotten the unconscious woman and his fears. But he hadn't. "Think a cuppa tea would help her, we've got some."

Roger said: "It would be a good idea if she wakes up, George."

He couldn't be sure that anything would help Daphne Mallow, short of fresh air, and a doctor; and he had to fight against his fears for her and for themselves – fears fed by the silence.

Why weren't they making some noise outside?

Then, rummaging, he found some sheets of notepaper and some envelopes; they were headed *Mildmay Ltd., Stationery and Office Equipment, 27 Butt Lane, Holborn, E.C.2.* Not far from here.

What was Ginn doing with Mildmay stationery?

Roger's nerves tautened.

Then he found a screw of paper, unfolded it, and found it was an envelope addressed to Gladys Domwell at her sister's home. It was in a strange, spidery hand of the signature to the letter to Mallow from Mildmay's; the handwriting of Netherby, the London manager.

Roger stood studying it, mind racing along new lines. He put it down, and picked up a bottle filled with white tablets, and a label, reading: *Nicotinic Acid*. He studied this, frowning, and then heard a thud, above his head, the first sound from outside.

George spun round from the kettle and kicked the methylated bottle over. The strong smell of the spirit rose, chokingly; the spirit wasted itself in the dust of the floor, the fumes rose, fumes which might catch alight.

Silence fell above them.

George dived for the candle.

"Keep that light away from there!" Roger cried. "Keep it away!"

Above their heads, the police, firemen, and a demolition squad from a nearby contractor were already working. They seemed to be moving at a snail's pace; men were actually lifting the bricks and broken concrete and twisted girders with their hands, or with small spades. Among them, Wortleberry was watching with dread in his usually placid eyes.

A woman, not far off, cried: "Why don't they get a move on if people are buried under there?"

Wortleberry knew the answer. Two policemen with their pick axes, and one newspaper man, were somewhere under the mountain of rubble. It had been pitched into the basement as if it had entered through a funnel; very little had fallen outside. In the middle, the level of the rubble was above the top of the basement. The rescue squad had to move every piece of brick and concrete with desperate care, lest they should cause worse injury to any of the buried men.

Wortleberry did not know what had happened to West or the boy.

He did know that the Yard men now at work seemed as much on edge for West's wife, who didn't yet know of this, as for West himself. But haste could bring greater disaster; they were doing all they could. A doctor and nurses stood by, an ambulance was near the spot; it wasn't a difficult job, the only thing needed was time.

A few miles away, sitting side by side in a cinema, the West boys were hugging their sides with delight at the antics of a great American clown, while Janet was wondering whether she could sit the nonsense through, and also if Roger would be home earlier tonight; and whether he'd found that missing woman.

It was pitch dark.

The boy sat with his back to the wall, next to Roger; and Roger was close to Daphne Mallow. He could hear the boy's breathing, but not the woman's. There wasn't a thing he could do. Though they were used to the stench of the methylated spirits, he didn't feel it safe to have a naked light. They'd have no hope at all if there were fire.

He kept thinking.

He wanted to see Netherby; was desperately anxious to see him now. Netherby seemed the only possible hope of getting a line on Ginn; might even have been party to framing Mallow. Ginn had killed twice, perhaps thrice; Ginn was at large, and Mallow might be hanged for crimes he had not committed. So, question Netherby *now;* every lost minute gave Ginn more time to escape.

It was a hell of a case, and would get worse if he couldn't send word to the men outside.

He could hear nothing, but knew that they must be working; the silence warned him how slowly they moved, how fearful they were.

The boy was dozing; one good thing.

He himself was beginning to feel stupid; the heavy smell, the thinning air; the weariness, were all conspiring. He felt himself nodding, and prodded himself upright. There was so much to do; so much the police might attempt; and every minute Ginn was probably getting farther and farther away.

It was dark outside now, except for the light of the car lamps and two mobile searchlights shining on the spot. Much of the rubble was out of the basement. Wortleberry watched three men moving small pieces away, with great care.

The light fell upon a buried man's leg; and on his hand. There was no way of telling whose it was.

One man, dead, lay on a stretcher near by.

A car came up. Chatworth's voice sounded, a woman answered in a monosyllable, there were footsteps, and then a boy said: "That—that isn't *Daddy*, Mum, it isn't, is it?"

Another child cried: "It mustn't be, oh, *no!*"

Janet West spoke in a very quiet voice.

"Come and stand by me, boys. There's nothing we can do."

"Come on, lads." That was Chatworth.

"Oh, isn't there," said Martin West, and instead of going back to his mother, he went forward. *"I'm* going to look and see!"

"Scoop!" Janet West cried. "Come back!"

But he was scrambling down into the pit, and towards the crushed and broken body. It wasn't his father; but it showed him what might have happened to his father, and he began to lift pieces of concrete away with the strength of a grown man.

While Janet, near the edge, had to struggle to prevent Richard from joining him.

That was at midnight.

At half past one they had the doorway clear.

c

Chapter Twenty

One Man To Tackle

Roger stood up, and gradually stretched his stiff legs, moved his cramped arms. He did it mechanically; something which had woken him from stupor, drove him to move. He didn't go far. He was conscious of the thick, heavy atmosphere, but it seemed to be inside him as well as in the air he breathed, something he would never be able to get out of his system. He didn't think much about it. Although he kept sipping water, his mouth was parched, his eyes ached, and his head was almost unbearable. He didn't think he could last out much longer. Nor could the boy who was still leaning against the wall.

Was George dead?

"Wake him!" Roger shouted. "Wake him." The echo answered. *"George!"* He bent down, and banged his head against the wall; then he stumbled over the boy. *"George!"* he cried. "Wake up!"

A whisper came.

"Wassmarrer?"

"George, wake up!"

"Wassat?"

It was all right; he was near panic, but the boy was all right; and better asleep than awake. He groped, found George's hand.

"All right, George," he said, "I was dreaming. Sorry."

The boy didn't answer, so no harm was done.

Face it: if they were going to die, the best way was to die in their sleep.

It was pitch dark.

Then, a miracle happened; or it was like a miracle. *Light spread slowly into darkness.*

The brightness came from a single spot, and shone through, just one tiny sliver of pale light, striking the moving dust and the concrete floor. It had shape, too; the shape of an elongated keyhole.

Breathlessly, Roger watched it; he heard sounds outside, and knew that he and the boy would survive; but now that it was at hand, rescue for them hardly mattered.

Was Daphne *Mallow* alive?

There were three boys, all clinging to Roger; three, where there should have been just his two. There was Janet, no longer in tears, standing a few yards away. Massive, ungainly Wortleberry was by her side, looking as if he'd been through an ordeal of despair. Chatworth, too, barking away at someone else from the Yard. Ambulance men were carrying Daphne Mallow on the stretcher towards the cream coloured ambulance.

The doctor followed them, carrying his stethoscope; as if a man couldn't tell life from death without one of those things dangling on his chest!

"Is she alive?" Chatworth barked.

"Just," the doctor answered. "With luck, she'll be all right. Gangway, there."

Chatworth was blocking the gangway.

The boys were clinging ...

There was the night, of sleep, and a bright new day. Roger woke to the ordinary sounds, and found it hard to realise what they were; the vacuum cleaner, of course; nothing must disturb the day's routine. Janet, God bless her! Janet – and now an empty bedroom, neat and tidy, with the newspapers by his side, and tea the moment he cared to shout for it; that would be as soon as the humming ceased. He sat up in bed, and remembered everything. He looked out of the window, then picked up a newspaper and scanned the stop press; there was no news of Daphne Mallow. He waited, until the vacuum cleaner stopped, and then called out. Janet must have been waiting for it, she was at the door in a flash.

She looked – wonderful. Flushed, wearing an old pink dress and a small apron, a plastic bathing cap over her dark hair, her eyes glistening. She came rushing.

A minute later, she drew back.

"It's all right," she said. "Mrs. Mallow's alive, she'll be all right. You saved her."

That took some absorbing, and brought a relief that was tainted only by the other fear; of trying and hanging an innocent man for murder.

"Ginn?" he asked.

"Chatworth rang up, half an hour ago, and said there wasn't any news."

"Netherby?"

"He says that Ginn wrote and told him that Mallow was swindling Mildmay's. Ginn wanted ten pounds for the information and proof, and Netherby says he paid it. I don't know the details." Janet stood back from the bed, and slowly shook her head. Something like laughter lurked in her clear grey green eyes. "I *was* going to ask you to stay in bed for the rest of the morning, but I can see it's no use. I'll get you a cup of tea."

She went out.

Roger called: "Any news of young George Smith?"

"Yes," Janet shouted back, "he played truant all yesterday, he's always playing truant. Instead of encouraging young rascals, why don't you tackle crime where it starts?"

She was only half laughing.

At the Yard, Michael Mallow looked much calmer than he had the previous day. He'd slept since he'd heard that Daphne was safe, his eyes were less bloodshot, and he'd had a good shave. He was just a handsome, worried young man with rather a weak mouth and chin; the type many women would fall for.

"I keep telling you, I haven't killed anybody. I did fiddle a bit on commission, but not much, I meant to pay it back."

"Did you see Norris at Reedon's cottage?"

"No."

"Anyone else?"

"Just the man with the bag. I've told you."

"Did you ever have any reason to think that Ben Norris was an associate of thieves?"

"No."

"Have you ever seen this man Ginn?"

"Never!"

"Ever seen *this* man?" Roger showed him a photograph of Chips Silver, and Mallow stared tensely, and then cried: "Yes, that's the man with the green bag, the man who was killed, but I didn't kill him!"

He stuck to that; and repeated his story of being knocked out, going to the cottage, seeing Chips Silver, being knocked out again – and waking to find Chips dead and the bag gone. He'd gone to the cottage and written to Reedon on Norris's order.

"Ever heard of a man named Rawson?"

"Norris told me he was Reedon."

"Hadn't you known Reedon as Rawson years ago?"

"No!"

"How long have you known Reedon?"

"Several years, ever since I went to Hoole."

"Why didn't you tell the police, when you found the body? Why did you run away? What made you take it for granted that the police would accuse you?"

Mallow said: "I've told you."

"Didn't you realise that by running away you'd only attract attention to yourself?"

"I thought you'd find the murderer, that it would be all over before—before you got after me."

"If you're lying," Roger said, "you're just making a noose for your own neck. You can take that literally," he added roughly. "How well do you know your London office manager, Netherby?"

"Not very well."

"Like him?"

"I hate the sight of him!"

"Why?"

"He's always needling me."

"Why?"

"Oh. hell," Mallow muttered, "I fiddled a bit on commission, fixed a few orders. I thought I'd be all right, if I held on—he's leaving."

"What?"

"He's on his way out—been fired," Mallow said.

"You sure about this?"

"Of course I'm sure. One of the girls in the London office told me. He's been with the firm several years, but he's been losing business lately."

"Did Norris know Netherby?"

"Well, sort of," said Mallow. "They'd met; Netherby came down to Hoole, and I took him round to the customers. About a year ago, I suppose. It was just like the swine, I had a date with Tony Reedon, but had to cut it. We had a drink with Tony, that was all."

"Did Reedon know Ginn?"

"I don't know!" cried Mallow.

Roger went out.

He didn't feel on top of himself, but didn't waste any time.

Wortleberry had gone back to Hoole, to take charge of the investigation into Ben Norris's local activities, but the real crack in the case started in London.

Roger checked every known movement of Mallow, Norris, and Chips Silver, and it led him to the Aldgate cafe. Silver and Norris had met there occasionally, the proprietor said; Silver had been going there for years.

"Ginn?"

"He used to," said the cafe owner. "'Aven't seen 'im for years."

"Ever see a man named Rawson—this chap?" Roger produced a photograph of Reedon.

The man studied it closely.

"Sure, but he was younger then. Used to come in with Chips Silver and Ginn, only a kid he was."

It was now beyond reasonable doubt that Reedon, as Rawson, had pulled off a big job, and "retired"; little doubt that Ginn had discovered that, probably through Norris, and planned the raid. They'd also planned to kill Reedon and possibly to frame Mallow – but *why* kill Reedon? They could have attacked him, or lured him away and raided the cottage. They'd wanted Reedon and Mallow both there together, if Mallow's story were true.

Was it?

Where was Ginn?

Had he got the green bag and whatever it contained?

Or had Mallow? He was in desperate need of money, which was a strong enough motive. Debt turned kindly men into brutes, honest men into criminals. Debt—

He was at his desk when the idea flashed into his mind. On the instant, he put in a call to the Superintendent of Police at Bridgnorth; a man he knew slightly.

"How well do you know the directors of Mildmay's?" he asked briskly.

"Very well," the Bridgnorth man said. "Why, the chairman is in the running for our next Chief Constable. Why?"

"Find out why their London manager, Netherby, has been fired, will you?"

"See what I can do," promised the Bridgnorth man. "I'll ring you back."

He was back on the line in an hour; laden with news.

"What have you got, Handsome? Second sight? Netherby's been systematically robbing the company for years. They took him on because of his accident, years ago, and he seemed first class. But a few weeks ago they discovered the racket. Being a decent crowd, they weren't going to prosecute, but—"

"We'll save them the trouble," Roger said, and his voice boomed. "Give me the details, will you?"

He was putting the receiver down when Cortland came hurrying into the office, for once more excited than placid. "We've got something fresh on Mallow," he said. "He's got a bit of fluff in Netherby's office—a girl typist. They saw each other on Sunday. How's that?"

"That's fine," said Roger, "that's wonderful. I'll see the girl first, and then face Mallow with her. Before we bring Netherby in, too, I want—" He gave an explosive laugh.

"The man you want is Ginn, remember?" Cortland said. "While he's free, he can raise hell."

"Don't I know it," Roger said, and grinned. "Remember those nicotinic acid tablets found beneath the rubble?"

"Yes," said Cortland.

"Seen the lab report on them?"

"Just nicotinic acid," Cortland answered. "Pure and unadulterated. Presumably Ginn needed them."

"Oh, he needed them," agreed Roger. "But he wasn't suffering from *pellagra,* or any of the diseases he'd need them for. Notice the symptoms after taking them?"

"Flushed face, uncomfortable sensation—something like a fever, I'd say."

"Could be," said Roger. He put his hand to his pocket, and brought out a bottle. "Here they are, anyhow."

He went out.

Chapter Twenty-One

A Finger At Ginn

Mallow's "bit of fluff" was a little girl, with a nicely rounded figure, fair, fluffy hair, and china blue eyes; and she was empty headed and scared. Roger remembered her pounding away at a typewriter when he had first been to see Netherby. She was in the waiting room at the Yard, quivering all the time, dwarfed by the policemen and by Roger.

She was likely to crack without giving a lot of trouble.

"Now, Miss Reynolds, it isn't a crime to harbour a criminal unless you know he is one. Do you understand that?"

"I—I—yes, yes, I do," she whimpered.

"How long have you known Michael Mallow?"

"Oh, a long—a long time."

"How long have you been close friends?"

Her eyes misted with tears.

"Not very long, I—I know I shouldn't have—have let him do what—" She couldn't finish; and after the outburst of crying, she was trembling violently.

"When did you last see him?"

"It was—it must have been Sunday."

"What time?"

"Well—well, morning. Mum had just gone to church. He rang me up, at home, said he was in trouble and had to see me. I—I met him on Hampstead Heath. I live near the Heath, so it was easy."

"What did he want?"

"He—he wanted me—" She broke off again, and the tears flooded; Roger waited with an impatience he found hard to maintain. But she recovered, and went on drably: "He wanted me to keep something for him. A—a bag."

Patience rewarded!

"A green canvas bag?" asked Roger flatly.

"Yes."

"Do you know what is in it?"

"No," she said, and began to sob again. "He tied it up, said I mustn't undo the knot. I didn't even try to."

"Where is it now?"

"In my wardrobe at home," she told him. "I haven't touched it since I put it there, honestly."

They found the bag, with a powdering of white over it – dust from the ceiling at the cottage at Hoole. Inside there were nearly ten thousand pounds in one pound notes, new ones which had never been circulated – nearly half the proceeds of a bank robbery now seven years old. Obviously Reedon had spread spending the notes over a long period, and made sure they couldn't be traced back to him.

There were also jewels, the better part of fifteen thousand pounds worth, proceeds of the same robbery. Mallow didn't hold out after seeing Iris Reynolds and the bag, and when he broke down he told everything. His story was much the same as before, up to the time that he had gone into the cottage. He swore that the man with the green bag had attacked him, that he'd killed him in self defence; and then had looked into the bag.

It contained money enough to get him out of all his troubles, to set him up for life.

So he had run away, intent on hiding the fortune until the trouble had blown over, hoping he wouldn't be traced to the cottage; but if he were, ready to say that he'd fled because he thought he would be accused of the murder of the man at the foot of the stairs.

He knew that Norris had posted the money to Daphne; Norris would have followed that up with a visit, believing that Daphne would know where her husband was, and to find out from her. It hadn't worked out that way.

Mallow had pretended to be absolutely broke, so as to lend credence to his story that he didn't know where the money or the jewels were. He had surrendered to the police, ostensibly for his wife's sake, actually in order to be away from Ginn.

He confessed that when the police released him, he had been terrified; he had phoned Norris to suggest dividing the haul, then been led into Ginn's trap.

"Norris told me what happened at the cottage," he said in a husky voice. "Ginn had killed Reedon, and Silver was inside looking for the stuff. Norris was keeping a look out. A couple of coastguards came along the cliff road, and Ginn and Norris had to hide. That was just after I'd gone in, when I—I was fighting with the man in the cottage. I got out as fast as I could, and didn't see anyone. Norris and Ginn guessed I had the bag. They thought it would be easy to make me hand over, but—but why the hell should I?"

He was almost indignant at the very thought.

"Is there anything else?" Roger asked coldly.

"No, but I didn't mean to kill the man, I tell you it was in self defence."

He would probably get away with that, Roger thought; and that was a pity.

"Do you still say you've never seen Ginn?"

"If I knew anything more, I'd tell you," Mallow said eagerly. "The only other thing Norris said was that it wouldn't have happened if Ginn hadn't seen Tony Reedon in Hoole, but until then I didn't know Ginn had *been* to Hoole. I swear I've never seen him! But—but listen, you've got to find Ginn. I'll never be safe while he's free. Nor—nor will my wife."

"I don't think you care much about your wife," Roger said icily. "But we'll get Ginn."

He said it as if he was absolutely sure.

He went from the Yard to Butt Lane, to see Netherby. Netherby had pointed a finger at Ginn, but Roger wasn't thinking much about Netherby or Ginn, on the way; he was thinking more about Daphne Mallow and her marriage to a selfish, callous brute. Mallow would undoubtedly get several years' imprisonment, although they weren't likely to be able to prove murder against him. At least when she recovered from her ordeal, his wife would be on her own for a few years, and perhaps be able to shape her own life.

The hell of crime was always the same: the effect on the innocent.

Now, he was going to see Netherby, who wasn't exactly an innocent.

Sergeant Appleby was also coming along, to take notes.

Netherby sat very still at his desk, with his left hand resting on the edge, and his right out of sight. The fingers were stiff and crooked, the hand looked claw like. Outside, the sun was very bright and the office could not have been brighter; even though his back was to the window, it threw Netherby's round, florid face into clear relief. His colour was so bright that it looked unnatural – as it had before. His hair was spread very thin over his scalp; here and there, streaks of the white skin showed through.

He was as aloof as he had been at the first interview, spoke only to Roger, and ignored Sergeant Appleby altogether.

"I have already told the police of my association with this person, Ginn," he said. "He offered what he called evidence that Mallow had been altering sales figures and drawing larger commissions than he had yet earned. I am not interested in the apparent probability of that—when a man is desperate, he will do anything." Netherby paused, to let that sink in; and when Roger didn't argue, he went on in the same thin, cold voice: "It transpired that Ginn was an acquaintance of Mr. Norris, of Hoole. I have already told you so. I asked Mr. Norris what orders he had given, and the figure showed a very grave discrepancy with the order which Mallow had sent through this office. I immediately inquired from other customers; in each case there are grounds for suspicion."

"Would you mind telling me why you yourself are under notice, Mr. Netherby?"

Netherby didn't like that; and didn't answer.

Roger glanced at the crooked hand; then at the hand which was hidden. Except by shifting his chair, he couldn't see if there was anything in that hidden hand. He didn't shift his chair, but Appleby, a silent witness, saw where he was looking.

"All right," Roger said, "I'll tell *you*. You've been robbing your company, and the directors gave you notice. They were too lenient, they should have charged you. If they had, we'd have had you before this—and would have checked your identity, Mr. Netherby, and your friends; especially Ginn."

He paused, but Netherby just looked vicious.

"Ginn was a really bad man, but he kept out of our hands for a long time," Roger went on. "He said he went to sea, and it was the general belief. But he didn't. He created a new identity for himself. Just as a man he'd known years ago, a man named Rawson who became Reedon.

"I don't know whether Ginn knew that Reedon was Rawson before he went down to Hoole and met him; but once he realised who Reedon was, he knew there was a chance that Reedon still had most of the proceeds of an old robbery. So Ginn plotted to get it. He was desperate, because he knew he was going to lose his job, and wasn't sure that he wouldn't be prosecuted. He had to make a big haul, and get away in a hurry. He had never wholly given up his true identity as Ginn; it paid him to be seen about sometimes. In any case he had a very helpful and devoted girlfriend, named Gladys Domwell. But whenever he liked, he could disappear as Ginn and reappear in the other guise.

"He had a hide out, in a bombed site near here.

"In his other identity, Ginn had gone to Hoole, on business, and apparently by chance met and recognised Reedon. That was when he decided to get Reedon's hoard. But Reedon *alias* Rawson had also recognised him as Ginn. Now, two people knew him under both his identities. Gladys Domwell was one, Reedon the other.

"Obviously, he had to kill Reedon.

"That was why, through Norris—an old accomplice who did a little fencing in Hoole—Ginn lured Mallow to Reedon's cottage. The whole job was to be done there—Reedon killed, Mallow left to take the blame. It didn't work out that way. You aren't surprised at that, are you, Mr. Netherby? Instead of sitting pretty with the money, Ginn had to chase Mallow, who had taken it. In the effort to set himself up for life, he had let Norris discover his second identity—so Norris had to be killed. His murder was planned so as to frame Mallow for a second time.

"That also failed," Roger went on, quietly.

"I haven't much time for Mallow, Mr. Netherby, but I don't think he's a murderer."

"I have never suggested—" Netherby began thinly.

"Let me finish," Roger interrupted. "There was some evidence which pointed to the second identity of Ginn—evidence which first gave me a reason for wondering what you could tell us. That is why I inquired from your Head Office, and was told the reason for your dismissal. There were two pieces of evidence—first, this."

Roger drew out the bottle of nicotinic acid tablets. Netherby's gaze darted towards them, then away.

"Know what these do?" asked Roger. "They make your face go very red. One tablet lasts an hour or so, and your colour gets very high, your complexion is very florid. But when the effect has worn off, you settle down to normal, and with skilful use of grease paint, or even dirt rubbed in, you look sallow instead of florid. You become almost a different man. You won't fool anyone who knows you, but the two descriptions wouldn't tally at all."

Netherby just stared.

"The second piece of evidence I am talking about was also found at the basement in the ruins, a place which Ginn used as a hide out. It proves conclusively that Ginn had special gloves made. These gloves served two purposes. Whenever he wished, they saved him from leaving fingerprints at the scene of his crimes, and, worn in his second identity, they created a feature of the second identity which was so realistic that he did not think anyone would ever suspect the truth. He felt so secure as his second self that he was both careless and overbold. He believed that, as Ginn, he could disappear whenever he wished. So as Ginn, he tried to get Reedon's fortune. In the process, he killed Reedon, Gladys, and Norris, thinking he was absolutely safe. He stopped being Ginn, and became the other identity. He hadn't got the fortune, but he was still free."

Roger paused.

Netherby sat with his body as still as his crooked left hand, his right still out of sight. But his right arm was moving. As it came up, and the hand showed just above the desk, Roger flung his cigarette case into the bright red face. Netherby saw it coming, and dodged. His right hand appeared above the desk, clutching a gun. Before he could use the gun, Appleby grabbed his wrist and twisted.

The gun dropped.

"That's fine," said Roger very softly. "That's the end of it all."

He was sweating; and felt that he had come to the end of a long, long trail.

There were good things that he could see. Daphne Mallow, with a chance to live her own life. Young George Smith, discouraged from playing truant, and fathered by the police. Janet and the boys, all their fears gone. These things did much to blot out the pictures of dead men and the sound of a tiny squeak as a woman died.

"That's fine," Roger repeated, and shrugged his shoulders, to straighten his coat again. "Harold Julius Netherby, it is my duty to arrest you on a charge of the wilful murder of Gladys Muriel Domwell at approximately ten fifteen p.m. on the night of Monday, June 8th. It is my further duty to inform you that anything you say may be taken down and used as evidence. Further still, I must inform you that the charge may be altered so that it may be brought against you in not only the name of Harold Julius Netherby but in the name or *alias* of Roland known as Lefty Ginn."

John Creasey

Gideon's Day

Gideon's day is a busy one. He balances family commitments with solving a series of seemingly unrelated crimes from which a plot nonetheless evolves and a mystery is solved.

One of the most senior officers within Scotland Yard, George Gideon's crime solving abilities are in the finest traditions of London's world famous police headquarters. His analytical brain and sense of fairness is respected by colleagues and villains alike.

'The finest of all Scotland Yard series' – New York Times.

Gideon's Fire

Commander George Gideon of Scotland Yard has to deal successively with news of a mass murderer, a depraved maniac, and the deaths of a family in an arson attack on an old building south of the river. This leaves little time for the crisis developing at home ....

'Gideon of Scotland Yard emerges as one of the most real working detectives in modern fiction.... A sympathetic and believable professional policeman.' - New York Times

JOHN CREASEY

THE CREEPERS

"The prisoner's hand was thin and bony ... And in the centre of the palm was a pinkish mark. It was the shape of a wolf's head, mouth open, fangs showing. Although it was what he had expected to see, Inspector West felt a twinge of repugnance a stab not unrelated to fear. It was the fifth time he had seen the mark of the wolf – the mark of Lobo."

A gang of cat burglars led by Lobo cause mayhem as they terrorize the city. They must be stopped, but with little in the way of evidence the police are baffled. Just how can Inspector West manage to do this in what is a race against time before more victims succumb?

"Here is an excellent novel of law enforcement officers, harried, discouraged and desperately fatigued, moving inexorably ahead under the pressure of knowledge that they must succeed to save human lives." - Cleveland Plain-Dealer

"Furiously exciting" - Chicago Tribune

"The action is fast, continuous and exciting" - San Francisco News

JOHN CREASEY

THE HOUSE OF THE BEARS

Standing alone in the bleak Yorkshire Moors is Sir Rufus Marne's 'House of the Bears'. Dr. Palfrey is asked to journey there to examine an invalid - who has now disappeared. Moreover, Marne's daughter lies terribly injured after a fall from the minstrel's gallery which Dr. Palfrey discovers was no accident. He sets out to investigate and the results surprise even him . . . .

"'Palfrey' and his boys deserve to take their places among the immortals." - Western Mail

INTRODUCING THE TOFF

Whilst returning home from a cricket match at his father's country home, the Honourable Richard Rollison - alias The Toff - comes across an accident which proves to be a mystery. As he delves deeper into the matter with his usual perseverance and thoroughness , murder and suspense form the backdrop to a fast moving and exciting adventure.

'The Toff has been promoted to a place of honour among amateur detectives.' – The Times Literary Supplement

Made in the USA
San Bernardino, CA
08 November 2015